Copyright © 2020 Tra'Niqua Francis

PRIMERA PARTE

LOS ZAPATOS DEL VIENTO

Saltó de la azotea del edificio, con los brazos abiertos como u
ave, y su cuerpo se sumergió en el viento, como volando por un instant
hasta estrellarse contra el pavimento, unos cuarenta metros más abajo.

La noticia me aplastó como si la piedra de Sísifo hubiera caíd
sobre mí. Por un momento pensé que todo era una macabra broma, d
esas que la gente hace en las redes sociales no sé con qué intención
Pero un minuto después recibí la llamada de Tanya para confirmarm
que era verdad: Mark había muerto.

Dolió enterarme de esa forma, como si se tratara de un extrañ
Pero él había levantado un muro infranqueable a su alrededo
Llevábamos más de un año sin hablar. La última vez que escuché su vo
fue cuando tiró los instrumentos y micrófonos y salió como u
desquiciado del estudio de grabación.

-¡Malditos! –gritó antes de marcharse.

Ese fue el final de nuestra banda y la última vez que vi a m
hermano con vida.

Aquella vez, me quedé en un rincón con el bajo colgando de u
hombro (ahora recuerdo ese instante una y otra vez, como una canció
interminable), pensando que Mark era un idiota incapaz de ver l
afortunados que éramos de tener un contrato con un sello discográfico.

Pero a él le importaba una mierda el dinero.

Sí, él pretendía encontrar "el sublime sonido y envolverlo en e
delicado papel de la poesía".

Creo que nunca lo entendí. Tal vez nadie nunca lo hizo. Tal ve
nunca nadie entiende a nadie.

El todo es que Mark está muerto y yo no sé qué diablos voy
hacer con mi vida.

Made To Love A Thug

Written By: Tra'Niqua

Synopsis:

There is always that one person in your life that will forever have a hold on your heart.

Trinity Lamb found true love at the early age of seventeen. Her newly found love was short lived, when one day the love of her life was snatched away in a blink of an eye. She swore she would never find love again.

Ten years later, Trinity has a promising career and has found another chance at love, or so she thought. Just months before she says 'I do' someone from her past resurface and gives her a whole new outlook at her future.

After serving ten years in prison Onyx is home and ready to pick up where he left. Which means getting back to Trinity. He soon learns that not only has time moved on so has Trinity. However, he isn't letting her move on without a chance to fight for her heart.

Caught between her current love and her past love Trinity doesn't know what to do. With neither man willing to let her go without a fight. Trinity is left to face the biggest decision of her life. Will she walk down the aisle or will she go back to the first man she ever loved?

People who are meant to be together, always find their way back. Yet, how far will Onyx go to prove to Trinity that she was made for him?

In this standalone novel you will experience the ups and downs of being made to love a thug.

DEDICATION

I dedicate this book to my beautiful daughter, Ta'Niya Francis. I love you so much, and I am so honored to be your mother. You will forever be my motivation to go harder.

To my boyfriend, Jarrad Brooks, thank you so much for supporting me and believing in my dreams. Also, thank you for discussing titles, models, and plots for my stories. I really do appreciate you.

ACKNOWLEDGMENTS

First, I want to thank the Lord for giving me the talent and ability to finally put my imagination to use.

To my personal test reader, confidant, and go-to person, Chelsea Simmons, I want to say thank you for dealing with me. I know at times I can be extra and nerve-racking, but you are right there to steer me in the right direction. Even when I start to whine and am ready to quit, I can always count on you to whip me back in line. You're always there to help or give your opinion, and I really appreciate you.

True love will never fade

March 5, 2009

Trinity

Walking into the hotel room, the smell of vanilla hit me instantly. I walked farther in the room, and my mouth fell open in amazement. The room was covered in long stem white roses, with the low sounds of Dru Hill playing in the background. This wasn't one of those regular types of hotel rooms; this has to be a suite because of the amount of space.

Tears began to build in my eyes as I looked around in awe. I wasn't expecting this at all when Onyx told me he had a surprise for me for our anniversary. We've only been dating for about a year now, and in that year, I learned he's not the romantic type.

I dropped my bag on the table, walked towards the door that I was assuming lead to the bedroom, I then put my ear to the door. The door was closed, and I was kind of scared and excited at what was waiting for me on the other side of the door.

Today is a special day for me. Today is the day I decided to lose my virginity. I still was having to fight an endless battle over the decision. At the age of seventeen, I knew I have no business being in a hotel suite with a man that is way older than me. Well, not that much older, Onyx is only twenty years old and is all mine.

Lord, if only my daddy knew where I was, he would lock me in my room until I was eighteen. Being the only child, my parents have always been overprotective; I couldn't breathe wrong without them losing they shit.

The door to the bedroom opened, and there stood my man. I eyed him up and down, taking in his appearance. My love was standing in front of me, wearing a tall white tee and denim Levi jeans. I shook my head and laughed to myself because, to him, this is what he considered dressing up.

"Babe, what is all this?" I asked as I leaped into his arms.

Onyx pulled me into a deep kiss that made my knees buckle. It should be a sin for me to feel this way at such a young age. Come to think about it. I think it is.

"Tonight, I want to be special with no interruptions. Just me and you. It's been one long year Trinity I have never felt this way about no female. Ever." Onyx said softly as he kissed a trail of kisses along my neck.

A moan slipped from my throat. I was trying to wrap my mind around what I was feeling. I love Onyx and was willing to do anything for him; however, I don't think I'm ready for what's to come after we have sex.

Most girls in my neighborhood lose their virginity to a dude who they thought 'loved' them then the next day he's on to the next one. I don't want to be like those girls, and I hope Onyx doesn't think I'm that easy.

My virginity is something I know I should only give to my husband. That's what my mama always told me. Yet, the way I feel about Onyx is a feeling I know I won't ever have again.

"Ummm…. Babe, I'm scared." I blurted out.

I stood there nervously, thinking that maybe he would be mad. The look on his face wasn't easy to read hell; at times, Onyx size could be intimidating. Standing at about 6'6 weighing two hundred and fifty pounds, most people say he looks like a 'more tone' Rick Ross but, it didn't make me any difference. I love every inch of him.

"Trinity, I don't want you ever to feel uncomfortable with me, nor do I want you to do anything you don't want to do. Okay?" He kissed my lips again, and I nodded.

I shook my head, yes, and he pulled me in for another kiss. "Okay, but what if after we do this, you feel different about me and never want to talk to me again?" I asked him. I bit down on my bottom lips, waiting for his response.

"Of course, my feelings for you would change for you." My heart dropped in the pit of my stomach as my worst feelings were confirmed. I quickly jumped out of his arms and tried to walk away from him. However, he grabbed my arm, pulling back into his hard body. "Aye, Trinity, where are you going? I wasn't finished talking."

"I scoffed. "I think I've heard enough." I tried to walk away again, but Onyx grip on my arm was tight.

"Calm down Trinity and listen. My feelings for you wouldn't change because you choose me to give me your virginity. The love and bond we already have is unbreakable. Adding this will only make us stronger as a couple." I stared into his deep, dark brown eyes searching for some kind of deceit in his eyes but, I saw none. I finally let the doubt I had in the back of my head go and focus on enjoying this time with my man.

I felt tears fill my eyes as I slammed my lips against his. Onyx kisses always took my breath away. I finally pulled away from him. "Babe, I love you." I kissed him again.

"I love you too, pooh bear." I giggled at my nickname that he'd given me.

His phone began to ring in his pocket, and it was if someone dumped a cold bucket of water on us. When Onyx's phone ring, that always meant he had to *make a run*. He gave me a look that read 'sorry' but answered then walked away.

Onyx never told me out of his mouth what he does for a living but, I ain't stupid. I see the fancy car he drives, the wad of money he always seems to have, and I know he ain't getting all that by punching somebodies' clock.

I can't complain too much because he kept my pockets full and I wore all the designer clothes. I am no stranger to money. My daddy is a professor at the University of Houston, and my mama is a head nurse down at Texas Children's Hospital. Being an only child, I had everything I needed and more. Whatever Onyx gave me was simply extra.

I let a loud sigh. I walked farther into the bedroom and jumped on the bed. "Oh my, this bed is sooooooo soft," I said as I laid in the big king size bed.

"I see you like the bed," Onyx said as he walked into the room.

"Yesss, I love this bed, and I want one just like this!" I squealed.

"Look, I need to make this run real quick, so get comfortable, and I'll be right back, okay, pooh bear?" I pouted and shook my head, no.

"Babeeeeeee, I thought today was about us! Can't it wait?" I asked.

"Pooh bear, I promise I'm not gonna be gone more than an hour, which gives you time to take a shower, find something in those bags that I got you which are in the closet, and do your hair." I jumped into his arms and kissed him long and deep.

"Okay babe, don't take long." I said as he let me down. I watched as he left out of the hotel room and as soon as the door closed, I squealed in excitement. Tonight, is going to be a night to remember for sure.

***

Looking down at the time on my phone It was a quarter past nine. I know Onyx said he had to make a run but, I didn't expect him to be gone this long. I moved from the bed and stood in front of the full-length mirror.

I ran my hand through my short bob and frowned. I spent

two hours on my hair, and it still didn't look right. Ugh! This is just going to have to do. I ran my hands down the little lingerie I put on for Onyx. The thin white bra hugged my small breast, the thin sheer lining covered my stomach. It covers the one thing that I was afraid of Onyx seeing. He says he loves me, but that's because he hasn't seen all of me. Onyx knows I don't like to show my stomach off because of the long ugly scar I had. It started from the top of my stomach and went all the way down to the top of my panty line. I never knew the real story behind the scar. Every time I asked my mama, all she would tell me is that I should be thankful that I was alive.

I ran my hand across my small, yet round ass. The thong was just the right size. It looked good against my mahogany skin tone. I didn't put much makeup on, only this red lipstick I bought that always made my pouty lips look fuller.

I heard the door to the hotel room open and then close. My heart began to beat fast, and my stomach instantly started to turn. I heard his footsteps getting closer and closer to the room. I took a deep breath and turned from the mirror as the door to the bedroom opened.

"Pooh bear, where you at-" His voice trailed off when his eyes met mine. The look in his eyes worried me. Onyx has never looked at me like that before.

I began to fidget under his intense gaze. "H-Hey where have you been?" I asked, trying to loosen the mood. The air was thick of a feeling I was unfamiliar with. *Intimacy.*

"You look fuckin' beautiful." Onyx expressed causing me to blush. "My sexy brown angel. Come here Ma'." He reached his arms out for me, and I slowly inched my way towards him.

My nerves were starting to get the best of me. With every step, I took my heart began to pound harder and harder. He pulled me into his big body then tilted my head towards him.

"You sure you want to do this, Trinity? We don't have to do

nothing you aren't ready for. I don't mind waiting."

"I-I want to do this. Just promise me one thing."

"Anything, baby."

"Just don't leave me or fuck me over. Please." I begged him. My worst fear is once I give him my virginity, he will leave me. I've seen it done to too many girls at my school, including my best friend, Kianna. I don't want to be just another dumb girl who opened her legs up for the first boy who told her he loves her. I refuse to be another statistic.

Onyx wiped the tear that I didn't even know had fallen from my eye. "I will never leave you, baby. You have a nigga heart in the palm of your hands. I ain't going nowhere." He kissed me, and that was it. The small fire I felt dancing around my body instantly became an inferno the moment Onyx lips touched mine.

His hands began to roam freely around my body. Touching my breast, my ass, and when his hands brushed against my scar, I froze.

"What's wrong?" Onyx asked, noticing my mood instantly.

"Nothing, it's just that…" I placed his hand over my stomach, trying to cover my scar the best way I could without him noticing. But, like always, he noticed every little thing I did. He grabbed my hands, lead me over to the bed then laid me down.

He eyed me up and down while licking his lips. He leaned down and began to slowly kiss the scar on my stomach. "Don't ever try to hide yourself from me. I love each and every part of you." Onyx said in between kisses.

Tears slipped from my eyes. I always felt my scar was ugly, and no man would ever love me because of it. Onyx lips finally reach mine, and it was like the world around us muffled out. My only focus was on him.

"Can I have you Pooh bear?" He asked while slowly making his way down to my most precious treasure. My breathing became labored, my palms began to sweat, and my legs shook.

I opened my mouth to answer him, "Yes." The minute that slipped from my lips, Onyx didn't give me time to rethink my answer.

He snatched the thong off then lower himself down to where he was eye level with my kitty kat. "Is she ready for me?" All I could do was nod my head. As nervous as I was right now, I just hoped that I didn't do nothing stupid to mess up this special night. "Relax, pooh bear."

Taking his advice, I relaxed and let this thing happened. Onyx rubbed the head of his dick up and down on my slit. I squirmed in anticipation as to what was next to come.

He put his hand on my stomach. "Take a deep breath from me, mama." He whispered against my lips.

Doing as I was told, I inhaled, and Onyx thrusted deeply inside of me, breaking the barriers that kept us apart.

"Ahhh!" I cried out in pain. "It hurts so much." Tears pooled in my eyes. I didn't expect for it to hurt this much.

"Shhh, I promise baby give me a chance to move all your pain will turn into pleasure, baby." He placed his lips on mine, and I accepted them. His kisses were soft, deep, and full.

With each thrust I felt us become more connected. The pain went away with ease, and the pleasure came full force. Sounds came from my mouth that I never heard before. My hands tightened around the sheets as I let Onyx take me from a girl to womanhood.

The things he was doing to my body should be a sin. I think it is a sin. Lord, please forgive me for my sins but, the way I'm feeling right now, I never want it to end.

A tingling sensation took over my entire body. My legs began to shake. "Something is happening. I-I think I have to pee." I told him.

He quickly flipped me over and filled me from behind. He was so deep inside of me it; it felt like he was inside of my stomach. My body began to quiver like I was having a seizure. A wave of pleasure took me for a ride. Tears fell from my eyes. I'd never felt anything like that before. A loud moan fell from my lips,

Onyx thrust became short and deep. "Damn, I love you so much, Trinity. This pussy is mine. It was made for me; you bet not ever give my pussy away." He moaned against my lips.

"I love you too." I moaned. "I'll never give your pussy away." I don't even know how those words were coming out of my mouth. All I do know is what I was saying was true. I could never give myself to another man. Onyx will be my first, last, and only.

"You damn right." An animalistic sound came from Onyx before he fell onto of me. "I love you so damn much, Trinity. I never thought I could feel this way about a woman before. I mean, I have never been in love before, and being with you now has me thinking about my future. Our future." He rolled off me and pulled me into his body.

"Our future?" I asked, staring into his dark brown eyes.

"Yes, I know you are only seventeen, but once you turn eighteen, I want us to get married."

My mouth fell open wide in shock. "You-you want to marry me?" I stumbled over my words.

He nodded. "Yes, I do. I know you have plans on going to college, and I don't want to get in the way of that. At the same time, I can't live without you." He confessed.

Tears fell from my eyes. Hearing Onyx profess his love for me like that made my heart overfill with love.

"Promise me you will never leave me."

"I promise Pooh Bear." He kissed me deeply.

I never knew he felt this way about me. I leaned into him and kissed him deeply. Nothing else needed to be said between us. He wrapped his arms around me, making me feel secure next to him as we both drifted off to sleep.

~ ~ ~

The sound of a phone vibrating hard against the wooden nightstand caused me to wake up. I was so tired that I couldn't even open my eyes. Groaning, I reached over to silence my phone. I didn't go to sleep until well this morning because Onyx and I couldn't keep our hands off each other. Thinking about Onyx, I reached out to touch him but, all I got was an empty side of the bed.

My eyes quickly shot open, and I sat up in the bed. "Bae!" I called out, hoping that maybe he was in the bathroom. I waited a minute before I called out to him again.

Silence.

Jumping out of the bed and I instantly noticed that his shoes, phone, and chain was gone. Those three items I know that he would never leave without. After checking the entire hotel room, I checked the nightstand to see if he left a note or something and got nothing.

My heart started to race, and panic slowly began to take over. Picking up my phone to see if he called or text me and he didn't. The only messages on my phone were from Kianna and my mama. Ignoring both of those messages, I dialed Onyx's number.

Ringing twice, it went straight to voicemail. I called him three more times only to get the same results.

I fell down to my knees, and all I could think of was the worse. My phone started to ring, and I answered it without looking to see who it was.

"Onyx?" I answered.

"Who? Trinity, where the hell are you?" I rolled my eyes at my mama's voice.

"I'm at Kianna's house; I'm on the way home now."

I ended the call before she could continue to fuss at me anymore. At this point, I can't deal with nothing else. I need to hear from Onyx. I just want to hear his voice, so this feeling that I have deep inside my stomach. Abandon.

Sitting on the floor and dialed Onyx's number over and over only to get the same result every single time. I want to believe that he is just busy with work and that he is going to call me as soon as he gets a chance.

I told myself I was overreacting that Onyx was going to call me. I told myself that for three whole days. Three days went by, and I still haven't heard from Onyx. I lived my life in a fog. All I did was go to school and come home. My parents didn't know what was wrong with me, and I didn't even know how to tell them what was going on with me.

How do I tell them that I gave my virginity to my boyfriend and now, my boyfriend is MIA? I don't think I can stand the humiliation of telling them what happened. Plus, I know they are going to be pissed at the fact that I gave my most valuable gift to the man who isn't my husband.

My husband, thinking of all the things Onyx said to me. He promised me that he wouldn't leave me. He even told me that he wanted to marry me. Yet, all that he told me was a lie. He said all that just to get in my panties, and now that he's gotten what he wanted, he's left me just like I knew he would.

My biggest fear finally came true. Giving myself to Onyx and him leaving without even a note. That's what hurt me the most; I thought I would at least been worth a note or phone call. Hell, he could at least send me a text message explaining his disappearance. He could have least given me some kind of communication yet; he chooses to just do this disappearance act.

Laying in bed, all I could do was stare at the ceiling as tears fell freely from my eyes. Sighing, I decided against my better judgment I answered the call.

My phone ringing pulled me from my thoughts. Picking up my phone, I watched Kianna's name flash across the screen.

"Hello?"

"Oh my God, Trinity, I have something I need to tell you. Are you sitting down?" Hearing the urgency in her voice, I became alert.

"What is it, Kianna?"

The line went quiet. "It's Onyx."

"What about him?" My heartbeat increased. The last thing I need to hear is something bad.

"Girl, I just heard that he got arrested for drugs and word on the street is he is going away for a long time. He's looking at least five or more years of prison time." The phone slipped out of my hand and went crashing to the floor.

My mind was blank, but my heart was heavy. Tears slid down my face as I tried to register what she just said to me.

Jail?

Drugs?

Arrested?

Were the only words that I understood. Unable to contain my emotions any longer, all I could do is cry. Cry for Onyx and our love. I could have taken anything other than this. Onyx going to jail breaks my fucking heart. Even with all the smiles, he brought me; I never thought that he could cause me so many tears.

I don't know if I will ever get through this.

Love isn't finding the perfect person

TEN YEARS LATER....

Trinity

"Damn, all I ask is that when I come home, can a nigga get a damn home-cooked meal, is that too much to ask?" I rolled my eyes and exhaled loudly.

Tonight is the wrong night for Aiden to be pulling this shit. Then again, what is new? He's always bitching, yelling, or complaining about something with his unsatisfiable ass. It was taking everything in me not to stab his red ass in his thin ass neck with a damn fork.

Fed up with his bullshit, I threw the take-out bags onto the kitchen counter. "Yes, it is too much to ask. If you haven't noticed, I work a demanding full-time job just as you do, and I still have enough sense to pick up dinner for us. You act like take-out from Olive Garden is so damn bad!"

"That's not the point, Trin!" He yelled, slamming his hand down on the counter. "I am yo' man! Yo' damn fiancé! You know as in soon to be husband! I expect to have a home-cooked meal when I get home. Is that too much to expect from my soon to be wife? Huh?"

I couldn't stop the laugh that came from my lips. I've had a long day at work, and I don't need this shit right now. If Aiden was a real man, he would take this damn food, thank me, and then go about his night. But, no, he wants to be a fuckin' asshole. I swear I'd be a fuckin' fool if I marry him.

"You know what, fuck you, and this food!" I yelled back at him, then walked away.

"Trin! Trin! Where the fuck are you going?" I heard Aiden call from behind me. I didn't even bother to respond to him. Not trying to stick around and end up doing something that will have me in jail. I snatched up my keys, purse, and phone then left out the house, slamming the door behind me.

I'm so damn tired of always dealing with his ass. Sometimes I ask myself why and the hell do I stay with him? Then I answer my own question because of my damn parents. They thought that Aiden was the perfect gentlemen for their only child. Little did they know Aiden was far from the perfect gentlemen.

Before I could make it to my car, my phone began to ring, I looked down at my screen and saw my best friend Kianna name flash across the screen. Pressing the green button to answer.

"Friend!" I heard her yell as soon as I put the phone to my ear. "Come over, let's have some wine, and I cooked."

"Say no more I'm on my way," I replied dryly as I got into my car.

"Wait, what's wrong?" She asked, picking up my tone. Kianna has been my friend since middle school. She knows me better than I know myself sometimes.

"Long story. Well, not really just the same bullshit with Aiden. I-I'm just fuckin' tired of his shit." I confessed. It's true. No matter what I do or how hard I try, Aiden always finds something wrong with what I do.

"Girl yo' ass ain't tired yet. Just hurry up and get here. I'll have your drink ready, waiting at the door for you." Kianna said before she ended the call.

I started my car and looked at the house I shared with Aiden. I remembered when we first bought this house. I saw my entire life with Aiden flash in front of my eyes. There was so much joy and love between us. We raised our family in this house and grew old together. Now, all I saw is a loveless and dark house, that's not a home anymore. And what makes things worse is I don't even know where things went wrong.

Letting out a deep sigh, I placed my car in reverse and backed out of my driveway. I know Aiden loves me; I just don't know if his love is enough anymore for me to stay.

Possessive Partner

Aiden

I stood in the front window and watched as Trinity pulled out our driveway. It took everything in me not to go running behind her and snatch her ass back into the house so she can cook me some fuckin' dinner.

She knows damn well I don't like restaurant food. We've been together for five years; I thought she would have gotten the hint by now. I can count on both hands how many times we've been out to eat at a damn restaurant. When I first met her, I told her from the jump; I preferred a home-cooked meal.

Being a VP at one of the best financial firms in the city of Dallas, I make well over a hundred thousand dollars a year. I provide her with everything that she needs or wants. I pay for her and her friend to go on shopping sprees and girl trips. Hell, I've even told her that she didn't have to work but, she insisted on working that damn job at the school. I know she loves her job as a counselor; however, Trinity needs to focus on what's important; Being my damn wife!

Trinity and I met five years ago at her dad's yearly Christmas charity dinners. I'd just graduated college, and my parents instanced I went. To mingle and meet people or for better words, kiss ass to find a job. The night was long and boring until my eyes fell on her.

Everything about her was perfect from her butterscotch skin

tone, long black natural hair, deep-set light brown eyes, and plump pink lips. She held my attention the entire night. I watched as she sat at the table with who I'd learn to be her parents and just stare off into space.

It was something about the miserable look in her eyes that made me want to know her. By the end of the event, I finally gathered the courage to go and have a conversation with her. From our first conversation, I knew she was mine, and within three months, I knew that she was going to be the woman I marry.

Fast forward to now, I don't know what has gotten into Trinity. However, a lot of shit is about to change now. Starting with her running away act.

I pulled my phone out and dialed the one person I knew who could tell me where Trinity was going.

The phone rung twice before she answered. "What do you want, Aiden?"

"Kianna. How are you?" I asked her. Kianna is Trinity's best friend and also my eyes and ears when it comes to Trinity. Anytime I need to know something about Trinity, I simply call and ask Kianna. She gives me a hard time at first, but she ends up giving me what I want because she doesn't want me to expose her little secret.

She let out a deep sigh. "Trinity is not here. I don't even know why you're calling me."

"You know why I'm calling you. Don't act like I don't know your secret."

"And you act like you aren't apart of the secret. Don't forget about that. Now, like I said, I don't know where Trinity is and when I do find out, I'll let you know." She shouted into the phone before she hung up.

All I could do was laugh at Kianna's dramatics. She better be lucky I don't have time to deal with her shit because she knows just how I can get. I logged into my phone and went into the app that I had that tracked Trinity's car. I might get information from Kianna; however, I can't truly trust her word. She's known to be a compulsive liar.

A smile crept on my face as the location of Trinity's car popped up. Just like I thought she was head in the direction of Kianna's condo. I closed out the app and grabbed my car keys. Trinity needs to learn that there isn't no running away from me. She's soon to be my wife and the mother of my children. I will be the only one she can turn to. She needs to know we in this shit for life.

He makes it hard for me to love him

Trinity

Finishing off my third glass of wine, I sat the glass down on the table and wiped the fresh tears that had fallen from my eyes. I've been over Kianna's house for about an hour, and I have yet to tell her the real reason why I was here.

"Trin, stop all that damn crying. Aiden ass ain't nobody to be crying behind with his funny looking ass." Kianna fussed as she filled my glass with more wine.

"I'm just tired. I don't even know where we went wrong in our relationship. Like is it me? What did I do for him to act this way towards me?"

Kianna exhaled loudly and rolled her beautiful hazel eyes. "Girrrl fuck Aiden!" She yelled loudly while clapping her hands. There is no secret that Kianna and Aiden didn't like each other. I don't know why but, ever since the first day I introduced them, they both showed their dislike for each other.

A chuckle slipped from my lips. I love my best friend, but at times her ass can be extra. We have been friends since middle school. We even went off to different colleges, yet, through it all, we remained friends. I waved her off. "Kianna, you do know that he is about to be my husband." I reminded her.

"And? You're still going to marry even though you're here in my house crying over him? What sense does that make? When was the last time you were happy?"

I took a sip of my drink and nodded. "Well yeah. I mean, I have already accepted his proposal; I've already started planning the wedding, and the wedding is only six months away. I think we just need to start going to counseling before we get married."

"Do you really think counseling is going to help? How many years have y'all been together? Five, right? How is that going to change anything? Please explain. Because if Aiden is the man he's supposed to be, yo' ass wouldn't be here crying. Period. Nothing more or less."

Tears slowly welled in my eyes. "Kianna, I don't think you understand. Aiden is the first guy I dated after -" My words were cut off short by the sound of Kianna's doorbell being rung. Kianna and I both shared a look. "Are you expecting somebody?" I asked, and she shook her head no.

She walked off towards the door, leaving me by myself with my thoughts. I grabbed my glass of wine and sucked it down. I almost said the name of a person I tried so hard to forget. The same person that I begged not to break my heart, and he did it anyway. I haven't thought or spoke of his name in years. The hurt he left with me is still all too fresh.

I went to grab the bottle of wine to pour me another glass when I heard Kianna's and another person's voice arguing coming front the front door. The other person's voice belongs to my so-called soon to be husband.

"Trinity!" Aiden yelled as he stormed into the kitchen area where I was sitting. I turned to face him. His bright skin was beat red, and by the way, his nose was flared I could see he was pissed. But what's new.

Exhaling loudly and poured me another glass of wine. I need something stronger than this wine to deal with his ass tonight.

"Trinity! Get yo' stuff, and let's go home." Aiden demanded.

I gulped down the wine before I replied. "I don't want to go home." I slurred.

"I said, let's go! NOW!" He growled.

"Um… Excuse me, Aiden, last time I check this is my house, and I didn't invite you in. Soooo you need to go before I call the police!" Kianna yelled coming to my rescue.

"I'm able to go anywhere my wife is!" Aiden shouted back at her.

"Wife?" She yelled in what she called her City girl voice. Last time I check, Trinity still filed her taxes as single, which makes her single, right?" Kianna smirked. All I could do was shake my head at her.

Kianna always want to start some bullshit.

I quickly stood from the table and grabbed my purse. I needed to get up out of here before the shit hits the fan. Both Aiden and Kianna aren't the type to back down from no one.

"Bye, Kianna, I' ma call you tomorrow. Come on, Aiden." I said, pulling him towards the door.

"Okay, friend. Make sure you call me tomorrow. Oh, don't forget we need to go shopping for our trip to Miami next weekend." She called out from behind me.

Shit! She wasn't supposed to say anything to him.

Aiden turned around so fast that I almost got whiplash. "What? Who going to Miami?" He growled.

"Listen-"

"Oh, Aiden, you don't know?" Kianna asked cutting me off. "You want to know why you don't know? Because Trinity isn't obligated to tell you anything you want to know why? Because you are not her husband!"

"KIANNA!" I shouted. "I'll see you later." I quickly grabbed Aiden's hand and left out of Kianna's house before anything else was said between them. I know my friend, and she was just getting started on her bullshit.

The walk to my car was quiet. Aiden hadn't said two words to me. I don't know if I should be happy or scared.

"I guess I'll see you at home-"

"You've been drinking Trinity. Get yo' ass in the car, I'm not letting you drive." He said cutting me off. His tone was low, and face was void of all emotions. I don't know how to read him right now.

"What about my car?"

"We will get tomorrow. Come on, let's go home." I didn't bother arguing with him and got my ass in the car.

The entire ride home was quiet. Aiden didn't bother turning the radio on, and I wasn't going to fight him on that. Tonight, has been draining. All I want is a nice hot shower and my bed. However, something told me that wasn't going to happen.

Aiden pulled into the driveway of our house fifteen minutes later. I looked at the house that was far from a home. It's like every time I come here; I dread going inside. Your home is supposed to be your statuary; however, this is my hell. I no longer see the happiness and joy I once saw when we first bought it. All I see is countless fights, arguments, and disappointment.

When Aiden I first starting dating, he came into my life like a breath of fresh air. He was patient with me; he understood that I wanted to take things slow. I had my heart broken before, and I swore the next guy I got with I would take my time getting to know him. Aiden was different from any guy that ever approached me, trying to date me. He was honest and upfront about everything, which is rare with men nowadays. Adding on the fact that he was fine was a bonus. His 6'3, muscular yet, lean frame showed his dedication in the gym. He wore his short with the sponge twist and kept his smooth baby face was void of any hair. In my eyes Aiden was perfect. He was in school, meanwhile working at his dad's firm. We would always discuss our dreams and goals with each other.

After dating for almost two years, Aiden and I finally made

things official. Shortly after becoming girlfriend and boyfriend, he purposed. One of the happiest days of my life. Looking back on that, I would have never thought I would be this unhappy.

My door opened, pulled me from my thoughts. "Do you need help getting out of the car?" Aiden asked with his hand out.

I looked down at his hand then back at him. I didn't bother to reply as I got out of the car. I wiped the tears that had escaped from my eyes. Thinking back on things, I can't understand where things went wrong. Every time I would ask Aiden where he think we went wrong? He would always say it's because I stopped being submissive, and I let Kianna in our business.

He always put the blame on me, and for a while, I believed it. I changed my ways. I became more submissive. I didn't hang out with Kianna as much anymore, either. I did what he told me was the reason our relationship was failing, nothing changed. That's when I realized that it wasn't me. I wasn't the reason the relationship was failing.

Unlocking the door and headed straight to the kitchen. I need a drink to help me with this overdue conversation I needed to have with Aiden.

"Trinity, we need to talk about tonight," Aiden said from behind me.

I grabbed a bottle of wine before I turned to face him. "Yeah, we do. I have something I want to tell you. Let's have a seat."

"Nah, I rather stand." He replied. "Say what you gotta say."

I took a deep breath and ran my hands through my hair, trying to find the right words to say. Yet, there were none. I might as well just come out and say it. "I think we need time apart. You aren't happy, and neither am I. That's not a good thing when our wedding is only six months away, so rather than calling the wedding off completely, I think it's best if we take a break." I blurted out.

I honestly can say I'm proud of myself for finally expressing myself to Aiden, something that I rarely do.

Aiden chuckled. "Take a break? Are you sure this is what you want to do Trinity? Or does this have anything to do with that little trip to Miami you and your hoe of a friend is taking?"

I frowned. "First off, Kianna isn't a hoe. Secondly, that trip has nothing to do with us!" I yelled. Just that fast, Aiden had pissed me off trying to pin the blame of our relationship problems on someone else instead of taking full responsibility.

Aiden stood in front of me with a stupid fuckin' grin on his face that pissed me off even more. I just stared at him trying to figure out where the hell did this Aiden come from. This isn't the same man I fell in love with.

I slammed the bottle of wine on the counter, getting ready to walk away and say fuck this relationship, but I stopped. I'm tired of backing down to Aiden for once I'm going to stand my ground, and his stubborn ass is going to listen to me.

"You know, Aiden, fuck you. It's over. I'm tired of your shit. I'm tired of feeling like I'm not doing enough. I'm tired of everything, and I'm tired of being unhappy. It's over." I snatched off my engagement ring and threw it at him. It hit him directly in the middle of his forehead. "I'll be out of the house tomorrow." I turned and left out of the kitchen.

My heart was beating fast, but I wasn't nervous. For some strange reason, I felt relieved. Just as I reached the stairs, I felt something hard hit me in the back of my head, sending me crashing to the floor.

"Bitch, you got me fucked up you ain't leaving me!"

I rolled on my back to see Aiden standing over me with his hands balled into a fist, and his chest was moving in and out rapidly. My mouth hung open wide as I just stared at him in disbelief.

"A-Aiden. I-I. . ." My words trailed off as I watched Aiden began to pace back and forth in front of me, mumbling to himself. I was trying to wrap my mind what just happened. I still can't believe this man just put his hands on me. Tears slipped from my eyes and down my face. Never in a million years did I think Aiden would put his hands on me.

I began to sob uncontrollably, causing Aiden to snap from his thoughts and rush to my aide. "Fuck, Trinity! Baby, please, I'm sorry." He begged as he quickly pulled me from the floor. "I'm sorry, baby. Please don't leave me, please!" I didn't even bother to reply to him. I didn't have nothing to say. I mean what do I say? Should I be like it's okay? Or should I say I forgive him? If I did say those things, it would all be a lie.

I don't think I will ever be able to forgive Aiden for this. Aiden picked me up and carried me off towards the room we shared together. The closer we got to the room, I felt myself starting to become numb. My heart was already torn between staying for leaving. However, now, Aiden has done the pleasure of answering the question for me.

I can give two fucks about how my parents feel about my decision. The swear Aiden is perfect for me; I wonder how they will feel once they find out that Aiden is a woman beater.

My tears slowly dried up, and my feelings were now void. I'm going to do the one thing I have been putting off for a while now; Leave.

Welcome Home

Damon 'Onyx' Warren

The sunlight and hot Texas heat hit me full force as I finally walked out of the place, I've called home for the last ten years. After being a prisoner of the state of Texas corrections for the last ten years, it finally feels good to be free.

I took a moment to inhale the fresh air. I prayed this day would come. Being locked up at the young age twenty years old, I'm coming home as a grown man ready to put these last couple of years behind me and focus on my future.

"Damon, baby, is that you!" I opened my eyes and followed where the voice had come from when my eyes landed on Michelle. A smile form across my face as I walked towards her.

I met Michelle while being locked up. I signed up for a pen pal program just to pass the time. A few months went by before I even receive a letter, and when I did, it was from Michelle.

Hell, it wasn't like I was getting letters from anybody else, nor did I have anything else better to do. My nigga Tanz tried his best to be there for me when he could, and I understood that. At least he was trying to do whatever he could to help me out. Unlike my entire family basically said fuck me the minute the judge sentence me to ten years. The only person I know cared for me is the one person I let down. The only person I loved, I lost forever.

I dropped my bag on the ground and picked her up as she jumped into my arms.

"Baby, I can't believe you're finally home. I missed you." She cried as she placed a kiss on my lips. Michelle has been down for a nigga for the last four years. She's been at damn near every visitation, she made sure a nigga had money on his books, and she kept money on her phone.

Out of obligation for everything she's done for me, I developed feelings for her. It's a plus that she's beautiful, smart, and independent. Thick in all the right places, golden-brown skin, big oval shaped light brown eyes, with sexy pouty lips. She owned her very own hair and nail salon in downtown Dallas. She has goals and ambitions, something I like in a woman.

However, the feelings she has for me aren't the same feelings I have for her. About two years into her writing me, she confessed that her feelings for me had grown past the stage of 'like' and that she's falling in love with me.

My first question to her was why? I don't have shit to offer her except conversation, nor could I do anything for her. I know I've been locked up for years, but, last I remembered females only fell in love with you because of what you offered them: not all females, but most.

She let me know that she wasn't like most females, and as the years past, I started to see it for myself. Yet, I just don't know how I can explain that to her that I don't love her.

"Me either. Come on, let's get out of here." I didn't want to waste any more time being here. I've been here long enough.

"What's the first thing you want to do, baby?" Michelle asked as we reached her car.

I shrugged. "Honestly, I don't even care." It felt good as fuck to finally be free. I don't have to check in with no parole officer or nothing. I walked clean out of jail with no papers. I did my ten years day for day, and now I'm finally free.

She smiled widely. "I can think of one thing we could do." She said as she licked those thick pink pouty lips.

"Hell yeah, let's go."

The last time I had sex was the night that I got locked up. I dreamed about that night for the last ten years. I think of Trinity all the time. I always wonder how she's doing, what has she become in life, and do she think about me the same way I think about her. Then reality of ever seeing her again hits me hard in the face.

I blew my chances to ever be with her when I got locked up. The one thing she asked me not to do to her, I did it anyway.

Michelle's soft hand touching mine snapped me from my thoughts. "Let's go, home, baby. I have something very special planned for us tonight." She beamed.

I kissed the back of her hand, "I like the sound of that."

The big smile she wore caused my stomach to turn. I'm going to have come clean to her soon about my real feelings, and soon. Before she starts to expect things from me that I won't be able to give her. Especially right not. My main focus is getting back on my grind.

My Man

Michelle

I shamelessly rubbed my hand up and down Damon's hard chest. I've been dreaming of touching him like this for the last four years. When I saw him walk out of those gates, all I could do was run in jump into his arms because if not, I would have probably clean smooth out.

I'm still shocked that today is a reality. The man I've been dictating the last four years of my time to is finally home. I kept sneaking peeks over at him as I drove. My stomach tightens every time my eyes landed on his thick brown lips. Damon is so fine, one of the finest men I've ever been with. Tall, dark, and handsome. Standing 6'6, big mysterious dark brown hooded eyes, you can tell he spent his years behind bars working on his body. His muscular body was tone yet; he still had a little bit of meat on him. His hair was freshly cut in a low fade. His thick beard connected to his clean-cut goatee that made his thick lips, making them look even more luscious.

I've dreamed about how his lips would feel like on me; every night, I pleasured myself. It's been a good seven years since I had any type of sexual contact with any man. I'm so ready to get home. Damon just don't know what I have planned for him. In the midst of losing my seven-year virginity, I also plan of getting pregnant. I know we have talked about having children, and he stressed how he rather be financially stable before having children. However, I'm thirty-two, and my eggs are slowly dying.

I even stressed the fact that I will carry us until he found him a job, but he didn't want to hear what I had to say. I understand that he wants to 'the provider' or whatever, but that will come in due time. Right now, I need Damon and I to make things official starting with having a baby.

I glanced over at Damon, and he seemed as if he was in deep thought. "Baby, are you okay? Do you want to stop and get something to eat?"

"I'm good just got a lot on my mind." He answered quickly, not offering nothing else.

"A lot on your mind like what?" I asked, pushing the issue.

"Michelle, look-"

"Never mind." I quickly cut him off. By the tone of his voice, I could hear the irritation coming out. The last thing I needed was for shit to go bad between us before we even start.

I' ma take what I learned from my last relationship and apply it to this one. I cannot let the last four years go down the drain all because I don't pay close attention to my man's every mood change, needs, and wants.

My last relationship broke me down to my socks. I loved the wrong man for ten years. I did everything I was supposed to do only to find out the entire ten years he didn't love me in return. In fact, he had a whole other family.

~ ~ ~

I rushed into the house carrying two arms full of grocery bags. It's fifteen minutes after five, which means I didn't have a lot of time to get dinner started before Drew comes home. And with the day I've had at work deal with those patients, the last thing I want to hear about is his dinner being late

As I rushed into the kitchen, something out the corner of my eye caught my attention. I stopped mid-stride turn and saw an unknown woman sitting on my couch. But it wasn't just the woman it was the two small children who were sitting next to her, who seem to be quite comfortable in my damn house.

I slowly sat my bags down, never taking my eyes off of her. She's beautiful; however, I have no clue as to who or why she's my house. "Um. . . hello who are you and why are you in my house?" I asked as politely as I could. I mean, I don't know how else it could come out, seeing as I don't know who the fuck she is.

She stood from the couch and sashed her ass over to me. I took a step back and held out my hand. "Uh, huh. Don't walk up on me bitch I don't know you." I warned her.

She mugged me up and down. "Ugh, I can't possibly see what Kendrew could ever see in you. No wonder why he begged me to move back home."

I frowned as I let the words; she just said register in my mind. What the hell did she mean 'he begged me to move back home?' Who the hell is she?

"Are you referring to my man Kendrew?" I asked, confused as to where she was getting at.

She scoffed. "Your man is my husband and the father of my children." She pointed towards the two small children who now I noticed looked just like Drew. They both shared his big, round hazel eyes, wide forehead, and fucked up hairlines. The part that took me out was the fact that they both appeared to be under the age of five, which means Kendrew has been cheating on me recently.

"How long have y'all been married?" I whispered. A part of me didn't want her to answer the question in fear of the truth. Then the other part needed to know.

"Kendrew and I have been together for the last twenty years, married for the last five. We have a total of four children. Ages eighteen, sixteen, three, and two. We took a break, and I'm assuming that's when you came along or whatever. But, I'm here now because he begged me to come back home, so here I am."

She announced so proudly.

I grabbed my chest as the pain finally hit me. Drew has been lying to me this entire time. What I'm not understanding is the time frame. Kendrew and I have been together for ten years. TEN! Something isn't adding up.

Tears burned to escape my eyes, but I refuse to give this bitch the satisfaction of seeing me cry. I reached into my pocket for my phone to call Drew because he had a lot of explaining to do.

Just as I was about to dial his number, the front door open, and his loud voice boomed through the house as he yelled, "Michelle! I don't smell shit cooking in this mothafucker!"

This is how he greeted me when he walked into the house. Thinking back on all his behavior, I should have left his ass years ago. I should have left him the very first time. Just as I was about to respond, the two children sitting on the couch jumped up and screamed, "Daddy!" Confirming that everything was true.

I turned and faced his wife, and the smirk she wore only made shit worse. I can't believe this man lead me to believe that I was the only one. I literary gave up my life to be with this man. I changed everything about myself because he didn't like certain things about me. Like, the way I wore my hair, how I dressed, or my friends. He even made me cut off my family. Claiming that they were always in our business. I swear I should have listened to my aunt when she told me not to move in with him. Yet, I didn't listen to her. Instead, I followed my heart, and now, look at me.

"What the fuck is going on in here?" Drew's voice boomed from behind me causing me to jump. I didn't have enough courage to face him. I watched as the children jumped down from the couch and ran to him. "Daddy!"

His wife slid passed me and walked towards Drew. "Kendrew, please explain to your little side bitch who I am. It's obvious she doesn't know the truth about who you really are. I feel bad because you actually had us come to the very home you share with her. The children and I will be HOME, wanting for you. I expect you to finish up here and be home with us by the time dinner is ready." The sound of them kissing behind me caused the tears to finally break free.

Our entire relationship was a lie. The man I fell in love with lied to me. The man who I devoted my life to lied to me. All the abuse I endured at the hands of this man for so-called being unfaithful to him, and this entire time he was the one cheating. I was getting beat because of his guilty conscience. How does that work?

The sound of the front door closing snatched me from my thoughts.

"What the hell are you just standing there for? Go ahead and start packing my shit and hurry up I don't want to keep my life waiting." He demanded.

I just stared at him. He had to have lost his mind requesting me to do something like that. I mean surly you would have thought that he would have offered some sort of apology or explanation but nope. That wouldn't be the Kendrew that I know.

I turned away and walked towards the kitchen. The man who I'd fallen in love with has turned into a man that I barely even recognized. I began to search the draws for something that I know that would make me feel better. My heart is broken beyond repair.

The sad part of it all, I think I kind of expecting something like this to happen along. I just didn't want to admit the truth to myself. I tried to convince myself that if I tried my hardest to be the perfect girlfriend that I can be, that one day Drew would grow to love. Ten years later, here I am. Broken.

I found what I was searching for and headed back to the living room where I heard the sound of the TV coming from. I chuckled to myself. I can't believe after this man reached into my chest, snatched my heart out and crushed it in his bare hands as if it meant nothing, just went on about his day.

As I slowly approached where he was sitting on the couch, all comfortable watching tv. I popped open the can of lighter fueled and began drowning him in it.

"Aye, what the fuck!" He yelled as he jumped from the couch. The enrage look on his face, a few moments ago would have intimated me. "The fuck is wrong with you-" His words paused when he noticed the box of matches, I held in my hands. "Woah, Woah, hold on, Michelle. Let's talk about this."

I tilted my head to the side and burst out into a fit of laughter. "Now, you want to talk about this?" I ask sarcastically. I shook my head. "You should have talked to me about this shit years ago."

"I-I know. But, listen baby-"

"Baby?" I yelled cutting him off. "You've never called me baby before. What has changed now?"

"Come on now, Michelle." I must admit that the nervous look on his face is amusing.

"You know fear looks good on you, Drew."

"Michelle." I raised my hand to stop him. "Please just hear me out." He pleaded.

Oh, how the tables have turned. As I stared at the man who I've given the last ten years of my life, and I felt disgusted, broken, and miserable. I gave this man everything that I could possibly give him. Only for him to basically said fuck me. He really thought that he could just tell me that he was leaving me, and I was just going to say okay? Yeah, Drew had me fucked up. He is going to have to pay me for my time, and I don't want his money. I want the only thing that could give me what I feel I'm owed. His life.

"Uh, huh! All the years I begged-"

"Wait, wait. I know what you want from me. You want me to confess everything, right? You want me to answer all the questions you have, don't you? Well I can do that for you. Just let me go upstairs and take a shower-"

I raised my hand cutting him off. I had enough of his lies and pleading. "I don't want to hear shit you have to say! When I was begging and pleaded for you to hear me out and what did you do? Huh? Ignore me. Drew, I gave you all of me, and all I wanted was love." I paused and let out a low chuckle. "And you couldn't even give me that in return, soooo…" Without finishing my sentence, I struck the match against the box and threw it at Drew.

"Burn bitch burn." Were the last words I ever said to him.

~~

"Michelle watch where you are going!" Damon's deep voice pulled me from my thoughts. I quickly snapped out of my thoughts and focused back on the road, but it was too late. I ran over the small animal that was trying to cross the road.

I cringed when I heard the bones crushing under my tires. "Shit. Let me pull over."

"Nah, just keep going. It's dead ain't shit you can do about it." I didn't even respond to what he said.

My thoughts were still filled with Drew. Till this day, I can't believe the lucky bastard survived. After he survived, there was big investigation. I thought that I was going to spend the rest of my life in jail but, someway somehow, Drew told the police that it was an accident. I'm mean, it's the least that he can do after how he broke my heart.

My break up with Drew sent me to seek a therapist. That's how I end up writing inmates. Well, she didn't outright tell me to write an inmate. She told me that writing my feelings down would help me cope, which lead me to get into the Pen pal program. I wrote to about ten inmates before I wrote Damon. After the first letter I received back from, I knew he was the one.

His letters were different than the others I received. The men I wrote only wrote back demanding I send them money, naked pictures, or just the dirtiest raunchy shit. Not Damon, though, he wrote me a poem and would go on telling me about what was on his mind and how much built up anger he had. He was just different. Different in a good way. Sometimes, when someone comes into your life so unexpectedly, it takes your heart by surprise, and that's just what Damon did. Damon is the man that I prayed to come change my life forever. I just hope he's ready for our fresh start together.

<h1 style="text-align:center">Enough of no love</h1>

Trinity

"Trin, baby, I need you to hear me out. I'm sorry. I didn't expect shit to go that far."

I wiped the tears that continue to fall from my eyes. "Aiden, just leave me alone. Look at my fuckin' face! How the fuck am I supposed to go to work like this?" I yelled at him. I'd woken up this morning with my eye was swollen shut and dark purple from last night's event. One look at my face gave me more than enough courage to pack my shit. I just didn't expect Aiden to still be here when I first came out the closet.

"Man, I said I was fuckin' sorry! What more do you want me to do!" He shouted, causing me to jump. His voice was loud and cold. All the more reason for me to get my shit and leave.

"What more do I want you to do? You know what, nothing I don't want you to do nothing." I quickly finished packing my stuff. "I don't have to deal with this shit," I mumbled as I grabbed my suitcase, slipped on my oversized purse, and headed towards the front door.

I heard Aiden yelling, talking shit behind me but, I didn't care. My main focus was getting out of this house without any more conflict. I can't afford another bruise like the one I'm sporting.

The ringing of the doorbell caused me to pick up the pace a little bit.

"Who the fuck is that?" He yelled.

What Aiden doesn't know is I've called for backup. Whether he likes it or not, I'm getting out of this damn house. I rushed to the door, turned the locks, and swung open the door.

"Mommy!" I squealed as I rushed into her arms, frantically. I swear I have never felt safer.

"Oh my! Trinity baby, what-what is going on here?" I pulled my shades, exposing my eye.

"Oh, my lord! Trinity!" She took a step back, getting a clear view of my face, and she lost her shit. "What the fuck! Awe hell, nah! Where is that mothafucker?" She shouted.

Aiden stepped closer to my mama, ready to plead his case. "Ms. Vivian I can explain-"

"Explain my mothafuckin' ass! What the fuck is wrong with you putting your hands on her?"

"Ms. Vivian let me explain. . . Ouch! Ms. Vivian!" In a blink of an eye, all I saw was my mama going across Aiden's head with her slipper.

"Keep. Your. Damn. Hands. Off. Her!" Between every word, my mama hit him over and over with her slipper. I was trying my hardest to hold in my laughter. Mrs. Vivian Lamb is a quiet woman until you fuck with her only child.

My mama is a small yet curvy woman, and seeing her beat Aiden ass with her slipper is pure comedy.

"I promise Ms. Vivian I didn't mean it. Ouch. Please." Aiden cried out like a little bitch. I just find it real funny how he's been all apologetic now, yet last night I didn't get the same energy.

"Mothafucker! You put your hands on the wrong one! Come on, Trinity!" My mama yelled. "I ain't finished with you, Aiden better believe that!" She continued to talk shit as she walked to the car.

I didn't bother to look back at Aiden as I got into my mama's car. I closed the door and let out a deep sigh. For the first time in a while, I finally felt free. I know I'm going to have to talk to Aiden again; however, it won't be today. Hell, not even tomorrow. I don't know when I'll be ready to talk to him again.

"Are you ready to go, baby?" I turned and faced my mama and smiled. I am so thankful to have a mama like her. She is more than just my mama; she is like my best friend. I can tell her anything.

"Yes. I'll just get my stuff later. Right now, I just want to get away from him." I wiped the tears that had fallen from my eyes. I can careless about all my material things. Clothes, shoes and all that shit can be replaced. My life can't.

The sympathetic look, my mama gave me warmed my heart a little. I looked back at the house and saw Aiden still standing in front with a mug on his face.

I remember the very first conversation I had with Aiden when our relationship became serious; I told him don't hurt me. My last relationship left me scared to even commit again. I had a fear of getting attached to another man. He made me a promise to never break my heart, and he did just that, and more.

***

Two Weeks Later. . .

Staring at myself through the mirror, I smiled at the woman staring back at me. My eye has finally started to heal, and I'm almost back to my old self. I say almost because I haven't mentally recovered from the incident with Aiden. I know it won't be easy just to let him go. We were together for five years but, I know if I take things one day at a time.

I wiped the sleep from my eyes as I made my way into the kitchen. The smell of eggs and coffee woke me from my deep sleep. One of the many things I miss about living with my parents.

It has been two weeks since I've left Aiden, and to be honest, I haven't even thought about going back home or Aiden for that matter. I've been focusing on my eye healing so I can go back to work. Being back home, I've been able to forget about being an adult. My parents literally have been waiting on me hand and foot.

"Good Morning, baby girl." My daddy greeted me, handing me a cup of coffee. See what I mean.

"Good Morning, daddy. Thank you if you keep treating me like this I will never go home." I walked over and sat down, where he already had my plate waiting for me.

"Speaking of home. When do you plan on doing with the house? I mean, your name is on the house just as his is. Has that no-good son of a bitch even tried to call you?" My daddy spat. I know he's mad because he was cursing. Something he never does.

I shrugged. I honestly haven't given it a thought. "Yes, he's called, but I haven't answered. Honestly, daddy, I don't know, and I don't care. If he wants the house, he can have it. I'm not going to fight him over it."

"I understand baby girl. I'm with whatever you want to do."

I'm glad he let the subject drop because the last thing I need is to be thinking about is Aiden. We both sat down at the table and ate in uncomfortable silence. My thoughts were filled with memories with Aiden and me. Both good and bad memories.

Five years together, and I can't figure out where things went wrong. I still love Aiden; however, things between us haven't been the best. No matter how much effort I put into making this relationship work, nothing happens. This time apart is well needed. I need to focus all my time and energy on myself.

My mama told me something last night that really stuck with me; the more I love myself, the less nonsense I'll tolerate. I felt every word she spoke to me; I felt that to my core. Even if Aiden and I don't work out, I can't let that get to me. I did my best devoting myself to Aiden, and now, it's time I devoted that same

TRA'NIQUA FRANCIS

energy into myself.

I will do whatever it takes to

get my woman back. . .

Aiden

"The number you have reached is no longer in service-" I pressed the end button and dialed her number five more times only to get the same damn recording.

"What the fuck?" I yelled out in frustration.

It's been almost a fuckin' month now, and Trinity still hasn't brought her ass back home. I gave her enough time to come to her sense because I was wrong as fuck for putting my hands on her. She didn't deserve that shit at all. I fucked up and lost my cool with her. I know she probably has her mama, daddy, and friend all in her ear telling her to leave me and shit. The Trinity I thought I knew wouldn't listen to them. Yet, it's been a month, and she has yet to bring her ass home only means that I might have lost her for real.

My phone began to ring, I looked at the name, and a smile formed slowly across my face.

"What do I owe the pleasure of this phone call?"

She let out a deep sigh, "You know exactly why I'm calling you Aiden. Why haven't you paid my bills this month?"

"Why haven't you convinced your friend to come home, Kianna?"

I could hear her mumble something under her breath before she began talking again. "Look what happened between you and Trinity doesn't have nothing to do with my bills. You should have kept your damn hands to yourself and appreciate her more than you did."

"Man shut up! Yo' ass don't know shit!"

"I know you need to pay my damn bills before I expose yo' ass for the lame nigga you really are!" She shouted into the phone. "I wondered if Trinity will actually go back to you once she finds out the truth."

I gripped the phone tightly in my hand. I'm getting sick and tired of Kianna and her little threats. If she knew any better, she would shut the fuck up. Because last time I check. . . "And that will leave you homeless and hungry, right?" The line went silent, so I knew I was right. "If you want to keep that luxury downtown apartment, keep driving that brand-new G Wagon, without getting a damn job, I suggest you convince your fuckin' friend to bring her ass home! Or else yo' ass will have to really sell that so-called human hair for real. You have forty-eight hours." I ended the call before she could protest.

If I know Kianna the way I think I do, I'm pretty sure she is calling Trinity right as we speak.

Friend or Foe?

Kianna

"I hate him! I hate him! I fuckin' hate him!" I screamed as I paced the floor, trying to do my deep breathing exercises that my anger management counselor taught me; however, the shit was not working.

Sometimes I hate that I can't tell me, Trinity, the truth about Aiden and me. It kills me every single day when I have to keep this secret from her. However, I know if I do tell her the truth, there is a possibility that I might lose her as a friend. Sometimes, I wonder if I would have told Trinity the truth when she first met Aiden would I even be in the position I am in right now?

My friendship with Trinity means more to me than anything in the world. She is the only person I have in my life. My parents and siblings all cut me off a long time ago, because if the life choices. Chooses that I am not proud of. However, it's not like I had an easy childhood.

My childhood is the reason why I'm the way I am. I experience things at the hands of my own blood that I should have never been exposed to at such a young age. I was shown that no one loves or cares for you the way you think they do. The only person you can rely on is yourself.

Looking down at my phone, I contemplated if I should even call Trinity. I hate that Aiden has put me in this position, to begin with. I wish I would have never met him all those years ago. I can't believe he's making me choose between my friend or my bills like I'm not about to choose...

Pressing Trinity's name on my screen and waited for her to answer.

Of course, I'm going to choose my bills. I love my friend, but I love money more. Sorry, not sorry. Although I know Trinity will never allow me to be homeless, I just can't depend on her.

"Hey, girl, hey!" Trinity sang as she answered the phone. I cringed at the sound of her cheerful voice. For the first time in a while it she sounded happy. I hate that I have to do this to her.

"Heyyy! What plans do you have today?"

"Girl, nothing. To be honest, I was about to just get dressed and go sit at someone's bar. My parents are driving me crazy, asking me about Aiden. Like ugh! Can't a woman just be a bum for a while." She exhaled.

I felt bad so bad for her because I know her parents are sticks in the mud. They expected Trinity to be perfect, and of course, they wanted her to marry perfect Aiden. Hmm... little did they know Mr. Aiden wasn't as perfect as they thought he was. In fact, he was so far from it; he was about two steps away from hell.

"Cool! I'll pick you up in an hour. We haven't had a girl's day in a while."

The line went quiet. For a second, I thought that she had hung up until she started talking again. "You know what, I would really like that. Let me get dress I'll be waiting for you on the porch like kids when they mama drop them off unexpectedly to their daddy's house.

"Bye, Trinity. I'm on my way." I laughed, ending the call.

I quickly sent Aiden a text to let him know what I'd plan.

Me: I'm picking up Trin. I'm going to take her out get her drunk; then I'll send you the location to come and get her.

Not even a minute after I sent the message did, he reply back.

Moneybags: Bet!

I feel bad as fuck that I have to lie to my friend. I just hope she understands that this doesn't have nothing to do with our friendship. As soon as I can, I will find her a new man. A man that will make her feel like the only girl in the world. A new man who doesn't hide or lie about himself. But until then...

Forgiveness?

Trinity

I swayed my hips as Megan, the stallion brand new song 'Hot girl summer' blast through the speakers at a new upscale lounge that Kianna ass bought me too.

The atmosphere screamed, grown, and sexy. Which I think was because this is a twenty-five and up place. I'm glad too because Dallas doesn't have too many upscale places to go to.

The bartender sat four more shots in front of Kianna and I. My eyes lit up like a Christmas tree. I didn't waste no time taking all four of the shots.

"Well, damn friend. That's like a shot number-"

"Eight," I said, finishing her sentence. "And keep them coming," I said as down another shot.

I am so glad to be out. I enjoyed my time at my parents' house but, the minute they started with the questions about what I am going to do next. I knew my stay was coming to an end. It also made me think about what the future hold for Aiden and me.

I just don't think I'm ready to go home to Aiden. I mean, would things be the same? Aiden did the one thing that I never thought he would do to me. I don't even know if I have the same feelings for him. Honestly, how can I? He put his hands on me for no reason. Blacked my fuckin' eye for what? Last time I checked, love wasn't supposed to hurt. However, that is all love has been doing for me. It took years for me to get over my first heartbreak. That pain was a pain I thought I'd never get over.

"Hey! Snap out of it." Kianna's voice pulled me from my thoughts. "Enough of feeling sorry for yourself. We ain't come here for all that. You are sitting here looking like someone ate the last chicken wing, and you had your mouth ready for it. Let's go dance!" I couldn't help but laugh. Her ass always saying some off the wall shit. That's why I love her, and I'm glad to have a friend like her. Kianna grabbed my hand and led me over to the small dance floor.

I pulled down the dress that I had on. I still can't believe I actually left the house in this. Hell, Kianna ass didn't give me no other choice. The skin-tight black dress I wore stopped just right under my ass. The cut on the dress showed more titties than I would normally like. The stiletto heels made my legs look longer. She was convinced that I was going to find me a new man tonight.

However, the thought of being with another man made me sick to my stomach. Yes, I only been in two relationships my entire life, but both of them have broken me in different ways.

"Here," Kianna said, handing me a drink. "Drink this and get your life together. I didn't bring you out for you to be looking all sad and shit. A fine as brother just tried to holla at you, and you were zoned out thinking about a nothing ass nigga who probably is worried about you!" She fussed.

Damn, I am really trippin'.

I decided to down the drink, put my worries to the back of my mind, and have a little fun. After the last couple of weeks, I think I deserve it. I've been told that I was uptight a time or two; maybe it's time for me to let my hair down.

After three more drinks, I was officially drunk off my ass. I picked up another drink only to have it slapped out my hand. "Nah, you've had enough. I'm pretty sure yo' ass can't even stand up straight." Kianna fussed as she texted away on her phone. I noticed that she had been on her phone most of the night. I wonder if she met someone new that she hasn't told me about.

I waved her off. "Who are you over there texting? Someone new?" I asked, changing the subject because I know damn well there was going to be no way I'ma be able to walk out of here on my own.

"Girl no. Just some nigga that's late on giving me my money for my bills. Friend, you know I don't love these niggas." I laughed, nodding my head because it's true. I haven't known for Kianna to be in a relationship except for when we were in college. Because we both went to different colleges, I never got the chance to meet him, but, from my understanding, the relationship didn't last. Whatever he did really messed Kianna up because she never got into another relationship afterwards.

"I'm about ready to go. Can you stand up, or am I going to have to find us some help?"

"Girl, I can stand up. Watch." I stood from my chair only to fall right back down. Gravity is not my friend right now.

"See what I mean." Kianna pointed out, causing us both to burst out in a fit of laughter.

"Hello, ladies." I stopped laughing when I heard the voice that belonged to my so-called fiancé.

I slowly turned around to see Aiden standing there looking good as fuck. I eyed him up and down and noticed that he was dressed as if he'd just gotten off work. The black long sleeve shirt fired against his well-built frame. The gray slacks he had on fit him just right, and I'm sure if he turned around, I would see his perfect sculptured ass. Hmmm. I don't care how good he looked; that doesn't change how upset I am with him.

I looked over at Kianna. "Did you tell him we were here?" I asked her.

"Girl no. I don't know why his bitch ass is here. You know damn well I don't like Aiden." She spat and I believed her. She can't stand Aiden or anything about him. If it was up to her, I would never talk to Aiden again.

"I was here with one of my colleagues and saw you over here."

"Hmmm. What colleague was that? A bitch?" I asked, sounding like a bitter bitch.

Aiden chuckled, showing off that million dollars smile I love so much. Ugh! I'm not supposed to like him right now.

"Nah, I was with the Nelson brothers." He paused and gave me a once over. I know he's probably pissed because I was out here, showing off what my mama gave me. Aiden always felt plus size women should expose too much. Well, tonight I'm letting it all hang out. "You look beautiful tonight, Trinity. Is it possible for me to have a moment of your time?" I didn't even answer his question right away. His approach was very different than I know him for. The tone of his voice was even different. His tone was softer. I guess those weeks away from him got his mind right.

I looked over at Kianna, and all she did was shake her head. "Don't look at me; you already know what I'm going to say." I nodded and turned back to face Aiden.

"Aiden, I'm not in the mood for no arguments tonight. I've been having a good time tonight and-"

"I promise it won't be all that let's just go to our house to talk." He said, cutting me off.

"Our house? Last time I checked we don't live together any-more." I replied. I studied his facial expression. Aiden's face always showed just how he felt.

He chuckled and ran his hand down his face. He showed little emotion, making it hard for me to read him, or maybe I'm just too damn drunk to realize it. "Come on, Trinity, your just being childish right now. We both know that both of our names are on the mortgage are on that house."

I eyed him up and down again and shook my head. As good as he looks, I can't even trust myself around him in my drunken state. The conversation he is talking about having is nowhere near my mind.

Exhaling loudly, I stood from my chair and stumbled a little. I hugged Kianna and thanked her for the outing.

"Call me if that bitch ass nigga does anything wrong. I'll be at your house ready to put a hot one in his ass."

"Okay I will."

After saying my last goodbye. I stuck my hand out for Aiden, he grabbed it, and we walked out of the lounge together. I took a deep breath and prayed that our conversation doesn't end like the last one.

~ ~ ~

"Trinity! Trinity! Wake up." I jumped looking around confused. "Hey, relax, you fell asleep. Come on, let's get inside the house."

"Why am I wet?"

"What?" He lifted me out the car, and that's when I felt something wet rolling down my legs.

"What the fuck, Trinity! Man, I know you ain't pee on yo' self in my damn car!" I couldn't stop the giggle that slipped from my throat. This has to be the most embarrassing shit ever. Tonight, will definitely go down in the books. I really do need to get out more. "Aye, girl, that shit ain't funny. I have cloth seats!" Aiden fussed as he picked me up bridal style and carried me off to the house.

"You bet not drop me!" I shrieked.

"I should drop yo' pissy ass." He barked.

I tried my best to hold my laughter has Aiden tried his best to carry me into the house. I noticed since we left the club, he has been more like the man I met in the beginning.

For the next thirty minutes, Aiden took his time caring for me. He stripped me out of my clothes, ran me a hot bath, and washed me up. It's been a long ass time since Aiden ever done something so romantic. I began to wonder how Aiden could be so loving, and affectionate then turn around and become a man I barely even recognize.

As he washed back, I had to ask, "Where did we go wrong?"

He stopped, then looked at me. His light brown eyes gazing into mine. "I don't know honestly. I've been asking myself the same question since the day you left. I don't know what has gotten in me. My dad would kill me if he knew that I put my hands on you. Hell, my mama would to. However, I can promise you that I won't ever do no shit like that ever again. You didn't deserve that, and if you never want to be with me again, I'm man enough to understand." I didn't respond to what he'd said. I couldn't find the words to say to him. I reached out and touched his cheek. I have never seen him so open and vulnerable before. This is the Aiden I'd fell in love with. The Aiden that would sit down and talk to me about our problems instead of fighting.

Maybe this is a new Aiden? Maybe me being gone for those two weeks made him realize what he has? However, the question is, am I willing to put the past behind us and focus on our future?

As he rinsed me off and helped me out the tub. He dried me off slowly. Giving my lady parts special attention, which sparked the fire inside of me. A fire only he can put out. He slowly wrapped the towel around me. All this special attention that he was showing me has me all kinds of confused. I knew that I needed to make a choice on what I want to do with our relationship. Do I stay, or do I leave? Am I really ready to let go of everything I put into this relationship? Pushing those thoughts in the back of my mind and focus on the fire that was burning inside of me.

I leaned forward and placed a small kiss on Aiden's lips. "I need you but, I don't want to be hurt anymore," I mumbled against his lips and ran my hands across his growing member.

In one swift motion, Aiden swooped me into his arms and carried me off towards our bedroom. Keeping my eyes locked on his, I was in search for any sign of deceit in his eyes. Before I go further with Aiden, I need to know if he's being sincere. My heart has been through enough, and I don't think it can handle another heartbreak.

"I promise never to hurt you again, and I'll do anything to make it up to you."

"Anything?" I asked, nibbling on my lip.

"Yes, just tell me what I can do, and I'll do it." He said as he laid me down onto our bed.

"Well." I started as I unwrapped the towel from around me. "You can start by showing me what your mouth is made of," I told him, spreading my legs as wide as I could.

Staring at me with wide eyes, Aiden dropped to his knees, "With pleasure, my love." Was all he said before he dove headfirst.

Three Months Later

Fresh Start

Onyx

Today is the day I've been waiting for since I walked out of those prison gates. Today is the day I open my first of many barber shops. When I got shipped off to prison, that's when I found the passion of cutting hair. It was a plus that they had a program in there that helped me get my barber license. I even took a few business management courses.

Man, it really feels good to see my dreams becoming a reality. My shop wasn't huge, but neither was it small. There are five stations, three 70' inch flat screen tv's mounted on the walls, and a nice sized waiting area. I also had a game room in the back that had another Tv mounted on the wall with the Xbox connected to it, a pool table, and a few old school arcade games for the little kids. The shit is dope, I swear. I just envision the shit; I never thought I would see it in the flesh.

The one promise I made to myself when I took those ten years was to never go back to the streets. The money I had in a stash, I was going to take that and make something of myself. I lost ten years of my life for what? Money and street fame, which neither of them got me anything behind bars. Most men go to jail, come home only to go right back to jail. I always said that I would never be that nigga. Jail ain't where it's at.

"Congrats, nigga!" My best friend, Tanz, shouted as he popped open a bottle of Cristal.

I stood from behind my desk and slapped hands with him.

"Thanks, man, but I'm not drinking this early." I laughed.

He waved me off and poured us both a glass. "I ain't trying to hear that shit. It's only four in the afternoon. This is a celebration for us both. My nigga has only been home five months and has opened his first barbershop in downtown Dallas. My nigga has celebrity clients and shit. Fuck you mean. It's too early for a celebration?" He shouted as he down his drink. "Nah, for real though. You then gave me something else to live for. That street shit was starting to get old. You came home and gave a nigga a new purpose for that I thank you, my nigga."

"No problem, bro." We both gave each other brotherly hug. Tanz is two years younger than me and one of the realest I've known my entire life. The nigga was more than a brother to me than my own damn brother.

I should really be thanking him right now if it wasn't for him, I probably wouldn't have the clients I had. Word of mouth is a mothafucker. I went from cutting niggas hair who I knew from the hood to cutting one of Dallas's most know rappers, and my clientele took off from there.

I was working every day, traveling to them, I was on call, the shit didn't even matter. I was hungry for the money and had to get it by any means.

"So, what's the play for tonight? I know you don't want to go to the club, but it's this new lounge just a few blocks from here. I heard it's supposed to be popping'."

I shook my head. "I don't know. I promised Michelle we would go out to dinner tonight."

"Oh, is tonight the night you're going to tell her it's over? I wonder how she's going to really feel once she finds out you got your own place and everything." Tanz reminding me of the thing that I had been dreading.

"Man, why did you even bring that shit up." I sighed as I walked back over to my desk and sat down.

A little over a month ago, I went off and bought me a house over in Fort Worth. Slowly, I've been getting the house ready to move into, and tonight is the night that I decided to move there officially.

I just haven't found a way to express that to Michelle. Since the day I came home, I made it clear that my first and main focus was to get myself together. She claimed to understand where I was coming from. Then out of nowhere, she started talking about getting pregnant and married. Having a family and shit. She took it upon herself to go to some damn bridal shop and actually pick out a dress. Then had the nerve to ask me for the damn down payment on the dress. That wasn't what really sent me over the edge, her going out and buying an engagement ring really pissed me off to the max. The shit happened a month ago when she came home, flashing that damn ring in my face.

I saw the happiness eyes as she looked at me, I heard the joy in her voice when she spoke to me, and she wore the glow of a woman who is happily in love. That's when I knew then that it was time for me to come clean and tell her the truth. I really do appreciate Michelle, and I will forever be grateful for her coming into my life when I needed her the most. I don't know where I would be if I'd never met her yet, I know deep down inside, that I can never be the type of man she needs in her life.

I do not love her, nor do I plan to ever be in a relationship with her. I just hate that I wasn't honest with her from the start. In the beginning, I lead her to believe there was a slight chance of us being together, married with a bunch of kids, but I was just talking. After I got my mind focused on my future, I knew what I wanted out of life, and Michelle just didn't fit the part as fucked up as that sounds.

"Aye, nigga, you will never guess who I ran into the other day," Tanz said, getting my attention.

"Who?" I asked.

I watched him drink the rest of his drink before he answered,

"Trinity." The minute her name left his mouth, my entire body froze. I haven't heard her name in years. Not that I ever really stopped thinking about her.

"Oh yeah." I paused, trying to find the words to say. Hearing her name just makes me feel things I haven't felt in years. "H-how she is doing?" I asked. I had to ask; I needed to know how life has treated her. When I went away, she was only seventeen. It still fucks with me that I broke her heart. I only wish I could ask her to forgive me. I can only imagine how life has been treating her. Trinity was very wise for her age, beautiful, with a good head on her shoulders. I'm pretty sure she is now married with a couple of children. Any man would love to be with her.

"Shit, she seems to be doing good. She was looking good, skin glowing, and shit." Tanz continued. I lowkey wanted to tell him to shut the fuck up but, part of me wanted for him to keep going. Then again, I don't know if I really want to know. The shit is confusing as fuck.

"Well, that's good to hear. Um. . . I' ma get up with you later I have a few errands to run before tonight."

We slapped hands before I grabbed my things and walked out of my shop. I needed something to distract me from myself. Thoughts of Trinity clouded my mind.

As I left out the shop, my phone began to ring. I looked down at the number and frowned because I didn't recognize the number.

I pressed the green button to answer. "Yeah, hello?"

The line went quiet. I was about the hang-up when someone finally spoke.

"Is this Onyx?"

I frowned because I didn't recognize the voice. I looked at the number again. "Who is this?"

She chuckled. "I figured you wouldn't remember me seeing as you refused my visits and never wrote me back." I let out a deep sigh.

"Brooke, what the fuck do you want, and how the fuck you get my number?" I barked into the phone.

"Don't worry how I got yo' number. I just wanted to call and congratulate you on your new shop. I'm happy you came home from jail and made something of yourself. I'm truly happy for you."

"Is that all you called me for?" I was unfazed by all that shit, she just said. The Brooke I know don't give two fucks about anyone except herself. Brooke and I fucked around from time to time. Once I noticed that she wasn't nothing but a money-hungry bitch, I cut her off and never looked back.

"There is no need to be hostile, Damon, that's all I was calling you for. Oh yeah, I almost forgot, I was also calling to let you know that I will be going down to the child support office."

I pulled the phone from my face and frowned. This female was talking straight out the side of her neck. "Child support? The fuck for?"

"Our eleven-year-old daughter Damiana Warren. Of course." She blew a kiss into the phone before she ended the call.

All I could do was look at the phone. I can't take Brooke's word. I need to figure this shit out for my damn self. I really hope I didn't get this girl pregnant because if her daughter really is mine, Brooke is about to make my life a living hell!

Just when I thought my life was on the up and up here comes my past...

Supposed To Be In Love

Trinity

I stood staring in the mirror at my swollen red eyes and busted lip. Tears poured from my eyes. I couldn't even stomach looking at myself. The pain I felt on my face and body couldn't compare to the pain in my heart. The woman who was staring back at me, I could hardly recognize. I can't believe I have let myself be subject to this kind of treatment. I used to always say; I would never be those women who allow their boyfriend or husband to beat them. Yet, here I am.

Beating coming from the bathroom caused me to jump.

"Trin, baby, come out and let's talk about this," Aiden begged through the door. I didn't even bother to respond. As far as I'm concern, Aiden can just leave me the fuck alone for all I care. This is the last time I let him do this to me. Last time should have been the last time, but, like the fool I am, I went back to him. A mistake I will never make again.

He knocked again. "Trin, please just hear me out." He pleaded.

I shook my head and turned on the shower. What was supposed to be a fun night out to turned into a night from hell all because of a discussion? A discussion that had absolutely nothing to do with Aiden.

~~~

"I really don't feel like going with you tonight. I'm tired, and
~~~

I feel sick. I don't know what's wrong with me."

Aiden walked over to me and put his hand on my forehead. "You ain't warm. What's wrong? Did you eat something bad? Do you think you may be pregnant?" I cringed at his question. Being pregnant is the last thing on my mind.

It's been three months since I decided to move back home with Aiden. My dad wasn't too happy about the decision of me moving back in with Aiden, which I can understand completely. I wouldn't want my only daughter to go back to the same man who blacked her eye, either.

Since I've been back, it seems like the only thing Aiden cares about is getting me pregnant. I would love to have a child with Aiden. However, right now wouldn't be the best time.

"Why are you looking like that?" Aiden eyed me suspiciously.

I shrugged. "Like what? I told you I don't feel good." I lied, trying to cover up the truth.

"I feel like you are lying but, I'm going take yo' word for it." He said as he handed me a bottle of water off my night stand. "I understand that you're not feeling good, but I need you by my side tonight. You know both of my brothers and their wives are going to be at this dinner. How do you think that's go make me look without you by my side, huh?"

I let out a low sigh, "Okay. I just don't want to stay long, and I'm going to eat before I go because I know Ashlynn's ass is cooking, and you know what that means." Aiden burst out laughing.

"You know what your right. We go stop and get something to eat on the way. Last time she called herself cooking that chicken was still bleeding."

"But y'all ain't tell her nothing. That chicken was bleeding more than a gunshot wound patient." I fussed. I hate Aiden's sister in law Ashlynn. She swore her, and her husband were 'marriage goals'; meanwhile, he has an entire family on the southside of Dallas. Yet, no one has the heart to break it to her.

"You wrong for that come on and get up," Aiden said as he walked towards the closet.

Finally, pulling myself from the bed, I dragged myself over to my closet. I took a breath before I looked at my full closet. Everything I thought about where I put it back, only because I know Aiden is going to have something to say about it.

My style is more reveling then Aiden would like. He prefers me covered or as he would say 'dress as the wife of a future CEO' whatever that meant. I've been dressing this way when I first met Aiden. I guess that's where the compromising in a marriage comes in at.

I settled for a light pink off the shoulder dress that stopped just below my knees. Aiden shouldn't have nothing to say about this because this is one of the many ugly dresses his mama bought me.

Forty-five minutes later, I was sitting next to Aiden at his parent's home, staring at the bloody, uncooked mess on my plate.

"Oh, wow Ashlynn, you really out did your self this time. What is this dish called?" I cut my eyes at Aiden's fake ass. I don't understand why they keep encouraging her ass to cook. Hell, I'm surprised Aiden's brother is still alive. Even their kids don't eat her damn food.

"This is something I found on Pinterest, then put my own twist to it."

"What twist was that not cooking this all the way?" Rochelle asked as she poked at the food on her plate.

"Rochelle, please!" Mark Aiden's older brother whispered.

I was trying my hardest to keep a straight face but, I can already tell this night is going to be fun. Rochelle is drunk, which means she's going to be on her best bullshit.

We all sat quietly around the table, poking at the food that was served to us. The only people that I saw eating was Mark. I actually felt bad for him because he had to eat this type of cooking all the time.

"So, Trinity, how's everything going with the wedding planning? Have you picked a venue yet? I know the perfect place, and Grace, your wedding planner, agrees on it also." Aiden's mama Beverly asked.

I tried my hardest not to roll my eyes at her. I can't stand this woman with a passion. I don't know if this is my wedding or hers because last time, I checked I fired Grace.

"I have found a venue actually, and I think it fits our guest count perfectly. Remember, Aiden and I both agreed on a small wedding." I reminded her.

"Small?" She asked with a frown. "How small are we talking because last time we did a guest count, it was around two hundred."

I let out a loud sigh. "And I told you I don't know two hundred people to be inviting to my damn wedding!" I snapped. "And last time I checked, I fired Grace. I don't need a wedding planner checking with you about MY damn wedding!"

"Well, you may not know that many people, but MY son does. Oh, and you can't fire Grace when I am the one paying for her. Trust when I say you can't afford her anyway." She fired back. Everyone around the table put their head down because they already know shit was about to hit the fan. Unlike Ashlynn and sometimes Rochelle, I do not let Beverly shoot her little slugs without saying something back to her.

Aiden grabbed my hand, "Trin baby calm down." he growled in my ear.

I snatched my hand away from him. I'm sick of him and his damn meddling ass mama. I then had all I can take from her ass. "Bit-"

"Um, Trinity girl, come with me. I have some bridesmaids dresses I want you to see," Rochelle said, coming to Beverly rescue because I was one second for tearing into her ass.

I stood from the table and walked away quickly before shit got bad for real. As I was walking away, I heard her say something to Aiden about me, and just like the mama's boy he is he agreed with her instead of defending me. And this is the so-called man I'm supposed to be marrying.. with his 'Yes mama' ass.

I walked outside onto the patio, and Rochelle had a glass of wine waiting for me. I took the glass from her hand. "Thank you but, I'm going to need something stronger than this," I told her as I down the wine.

"Girl, you know this all her ass have in here. She too busy trying to be so damn high class she needs to do better buying them dry ass wigs."

We both shared a laugh. I know I can always count on Rochelle to make me laugh.

She filled my glass with more wine. "How do you do it? I mean, you and Mark have been together for fifteen years. I don't know if I can deal with her ass for that long without going upside her head."

"Chileeeee, all I can say it takes a lot of patience. She is the main reason Mark and I went straight to the courthouse to get married. Yeah, I wanted a big wedding, but I didn't want the headache with her. She is just too damn extra. But, if your love for Aiden is strong, you can overlook all her foolishness."

I chuckled as I took another sip of my wine. "I don't think our long is that strong. I don't know how much more I can deal with Aiden and his bullshit."

She waved me off. "Girl, you just saying that because of your monster in law. Trust me when I say I felt the same way you do now."

I down the rest of my wine and thought about what she just said. Is this something that Aiden and I can overcome? Hell, our relationship is still semi kind of rocky. Adding on this shit with his mama, I don't know how much more I can take. It would be okay if she just talked shit behind my back like regular people, but, nah, she wants to be disrespectful like I won't say something to her. I don't like negativity or drama, and lately, that has been all that has been around me.

"Girl, I remember when Mark and I separated for about two months. He stayed here. The entire time he was here, Beverly was in his ear telling him to take our children and divorce me. Now, you would think she would encourage him to go home and make his marriage, right? Nope."

I couldn't help the laugh that slipped from my mouth. I knew Beverly to be something else but, this is too much.

"I wish she would do some shit like that to me. I wouldn't even fight her. Hell, if you want your son to divorce me, then fine. Hell set me free from this fucked up family."

"What?"

We both jumped at the sound of Aiden's voice. I turned around to see him standing there with a mean mug on his face, and his nose flared. I don't know how much he heard.

"Um… Aiden, how long you been standing there?" Rochelle asked, trying to break the silence, but it was no use. Obviously, Aiden heard something he didn't like because he stood in the same spot, not saying nothing.

I rolled my eyes and down the rest of my wine. It's about to be a long night. Aiden walked over to me, grabbed my arm roughly, "Let's go Amina."

"Wait a minute Aiden; you don't have to pull on her like that!" Rochelle yelled, but Aiden didn't pay her no mind.

"Aiden, slow down, you're hurting me!" I cried out.

I tried my hardest to pull away from him, but the tight grip he had on me made it hard. "Shut the fuck up! I've had all I can take of your mouth today." He growled.

"My mouth? Your crooked wig-wearing mama-"

WHAM! WHAM!

Before I could even finish my sentence, Aiden slapped me hard across my face sending me crashing to the ground.

"Get the fuck in the car and hurry up! I ain't finished with yo' ass yet just wait til we get home." Fear took over when I saw the killer look in Aiden's eyes. I know that this night isn't going to end well.

BOOM! BOOM! BOOM!

I jumped at the loud knocks coming from the bathroom door. "Trinity, baby, please let me in. Let's just talk about this." Aiden called from the other side of the door.

I looked back at my reflection and cringed at what I saw. "At least this time he didn't black my eye." I chuckled to myself. More tears fell from my eyes.

What am I thinking? I can't believe I was making jokes about this. This is not the life I want for myself. I am not the woman whose boyfriend beats her up. I don't care how much I love Aiden; I refuse to be someone's punching bag.

I wiped the tears that fell from my face, took a deep breath before I walked out of the bathroom. I opened the door, and there stood Aiden with the look of remorse written all over his face.

"Damn, Trin. I didn't mean to go that far-"

I raised my hand, cutting him off. I'd enough of the sad-ass apologizes. This is the end of us. There is no coming back from this. Sometimes your heart needs more time to accept what your mind already knows. I love him with all my heart; however, I love myself more.

I pushed him out my way and headed straight out of the bedroom. I didn't bother to explain shit to Aiden. At the end of the day, we aren't married, and I don't have to put up with this shit.

"Trinity! Talk to me!" I stopped in my tracks and turned to face him.

"We have nothing–"

Aiden dropped to his knees and buried his face into my stomach. "Baby, please don't leave me. I'll do anything. I'll go to counseling, anger management, wherever just don't leave me, please!" He cried out. The sight in front of me left me speechless. Never have I ever seen Aiden act this way. He's on his knees crying, begging me not to leave.

I stood stuck in the same spot, confused with a million questions running through my head. Will Aiden really change? Can we really make this work? Will he really seek the help he needs? Will he stop putting his hands on me?

Yes, I do love Aiden but...

"Trinity baby, are you going to leave me?"

"I-I."

"Please, baby, I promise to never put my hands on you again. You can even come to counseling with me, and if it's about my mama, I will deal with her. Anything for you, Trinity, I just don't think I can handle you leaving me again. I love you, and I need you just like I need air to breathe." He confessed.

Tears burned my eyes as I stared into his brown eyes. I searched for any sign of a lie and saw none. All the thoughts of leaving Aiden went out of the window. I fell to the ground in front of him.

"I love you. But Aiden." I used my hand to lift his head and pointed to my busted lip. "Look at my face. How can you expect me to stay?"

"Baby listen–"

I raised my hand, cutting him off. "No, you listen. I thought the last time you put your hands on me was the last time. I am no one's punching bag. I don't deserve none of this. I'm willing to put in the work to make this work, but you are going to have to go get help. Especially if you want to marry me, our wedding is set in six months; that's how long you have to get yo' shit together because I refuse to marry a woman beater." I told him.

"I'm sorry, Trinity, and I'm willing to do whatever I need to do in order to make us work. Thank you for giving me another chance. I promise to be a better man for you."

I heard what Aiden was saying, and I want to believe him. I just hope he actually means what he says, and I don't regret staying.

Broken Promises

Onyx

I sat across the table from Michelle in this five-star restaurant she's been dying to go to. I couldn't focus on the menu because I was trying to find the words to break up with Michelle. I've been putting off this for far too long now. I wasn't expecting to do this shit out in public like this but, when I called her and told her we needed to talk, she insisted that we meet here. I'm probably going to regret this later.

She sat there beautiful as ever. I can tell she took her time getting dressed. Her hair was freshly done, cut real short for her style, her make-up was flawless, and the red strapless dress hugged all her small curves. Damn, this shit is going to be harder than I expected.

"Did you figure out what you wanted yet?"

I heard her talking, but my mind was focused on her lips. The red lipstick she wore made her lips look fuller against her bourbon skin tone.

"Bae!" She kicked me to get my attention.

"Huh? Um. . . Nah, not yet. Michelle, we need to talk." I told her as I laid my menu down on the table.

She gave me a weird look. "Um. . . Okayyyy, about what bae?"

I took a deep breath before I started. I know this isn't going to end well; still, this is something that has to be done. I know she has noticed the change between us. I barley went to her house anymore because I had my own. She never questioned me about it. Maybe she thought I was staying nights at my shop. Then again, maybe she didn't care and had her own thing going on. Because I haven't touched her since the day I came home. It's been months!

I grabbed her hand and stared into her eyes. As much as I hate to do this, "You know how much I appreciate you. How you held me down while I was locked down when I had no one else to turn too." I paused and took a deep breath. "The feelings I have you aren't what you think they are."

She snatched her hand away from me, and I watched her face fall into a frown. "What are you trying to say, because I know it's not what I think it is?" The tone of her voice let me know that she was pissed.

I reached for her hand again; she folded them across her chest.

"I have feelings for you, Michelle, I do. Just not the type of feelings you expect me too."

She scoffed. "Expect? Last time I checked, you told me you loved me!"

"I never said I loved you. I would always you too." I corrected her.

I cursed myself as I watched the tears form in her eyes. I never meant for things to go as far as they have with Michelle. "But… But I love you." She whispered with tears falling from her eyes. "You really doing this here? I mean, you couldn't wait?"

I shook my head. I've waited to do this long enough. If I didn't do this now, I know I won't ever do it. "Michelle, please understand that I never met for things to go this far."

"Really? I can't tell! I mean, when were you going to stop? Was it after the weekly hundred dollars I was putting on the phone? Was it the two hundred dollars I kept on your books? I mean, tell me something Damon because right now, I don't understand shit, you say." She raged.

I chuckled and sat back in my chair. I knew this shit was going to come up. "Would you prefer me to get out and ghost yo' ass? Would that be better?"

"No-"

"That's what the fuck I thought!" I snapped, cutting her off.

Something told me this was going to be her reaction, which was why I came prepared here. One thing my grandpa taught me, that as a man, you never leave this earth owing no one no money. Always pay your debts. I dug into my pocket and pulled out a check made out to her with the money I owed her plus interest. I slowly slid it across the table. Once she realized what it was, I could have sworn I saw smoke coming from her ears.

"Really? Is this how you do me? After all these years of holding you down, pushing you to do better, all I get is a fuckin' check!" She yelled, making a scene.

"Michelle-" My words were cut off when she threw her drink in my face. I counted backward from ten to keep myself calm. The last thing I needed was to spaz the fuck out on her.

"Fuck you, Damon. I promise you will regret this!" She yelled before she stormed out of the restaurant.

There was no point in following behind her. What is done is done. I just wished shit could have ended better than this. Michelle is a cool person, and I wouldn't mind being friends; however, I don't know if she will feel the same way.

The waiter finally came over with some napkins. "Sir, is there anything that I can do for you?"

I shook my head and handed her a couple of twenties before I stood to leave. As I was walking out of the restaurant, a familiar laugh caught my attention. I turned to follow the sound of her voice, and the minute my eyes fell on her, my breath got stuck in my throat.

She looked the same as I remember only more grown. Her smile, her laugh, the light that she carried in her eyes that I remembered. I was drawn to her like metal to a metal detector. I walked over to where she was sitting at the bar. The closer I got, the more nervous I became.

What will I say? It's been years since I saw her, and I did the one thing she promised me not to do. Break her heart.

That was years ago, we were kids, and there is nothing wrong with saying hello, right?

I walked up to her and her friend while they were in deep conversation. I was still in awe at how beautiful she has grown to be. I mean, what am I saying. She has always been beautiful.

I cleared my throat, getting their attention. Simultaneously she and her friend turned to face me. A smile crept on my face as I watched her eyes widen.

"Onyx." She whispered.

"Hello, Trinity."

True love has a habit of coming back

Kianna insisted that we go out to this new happy hour spot downtown. I really didn't feel like being out and about. But it's been a while since we've had our girl time. I have been so caught up with Aiden that I have been neglecting my best friend.

Speaking of Aiden, he has sure made a drastic change all in a couple of days. He's doing little stuff like asking me if I feel like cooking instead of demanding it. He has also started this thing where he wanted us to express ourselves without the other person getting upset. It's only been a couple of days, so I just hope that he continues this the last thing we both need is for him to revert to his old ways.

A text notification went off on my phone. I looked down at the screen and smiled at the emoji blowing a kiss that Aiden sent me. I sent him one back.

"Girl, would you get off that phone texting that funny lookin' nigga. You supposed to be spending time with me!" Kianna pouted.

I slid my phone back into my small clutch purse. "I'm sorry, friend. You have all my attention now! What's been new? Any new men in your life?" I asked as I took a sip of long island iced tea.

She rolled her eyes and downed her shot of Hennessey. "Unlike you, I don't love these niggas. I use them for their money."

"Kianna, when are you going to settle down?"

She began to cough uncontrollably. "Bitch never! You know I am not the settling down type you know after the one relationship I had in college that was it for me."

"You never told me what really happened between you and that guy."

She shrugged. "I fell in love with him, and he broke my damn heart. The end." She said as she downed another shot. I shook my head because something more had to happen to act this way. The Kianna I knew before college wasn't this bitter and broken. She was bubbly and adventurous. Whoever the guy was she was in love with broke more than her heart; he also broke her sprit.

Leaving the conversation alone because I can sense her attitude. The last thing I want is to upset her on our girl's date. Instead, I focused on regular girl talk and enjoying some good drinks and food.

Two hours later, we were laughing and having a good ole' time like we used to. It's been such a long time since we have had this time together.

"Friend, I really miss you," I told her.

"Same friend, same."

"We need-"

Someone clearing their throat behind me got my attention. I turned around and almost fell off the stool.

"Onyx," I whispered. My mouth instantly went dry. I eyed him from head to toe in awe that he was standing in front of me. The last time I saw him was when I gave him my virginity, and he broke my heart.

"Hello, Trinity." He said with a wide smile showing off all white of his thirty-two teeth. I sat there in shock that he was even in front of me right now, looking better than ever. Taking in his body, I must say jail has done his body some good.

Just him standing here in front of me caused a wave of emotions and feelings. Things that I haven't felt in a long time. This that I thought I buried when I found out that Onyx was going to jail.

My stomach began to cramp, and everything I'd just eaten and drank felt like it was about to come up. I opened my mouth but quickly slapped my hand across my mouth then rushed off to the restroom. I ran into the restroom into the first empty stall and began to throw up all the contents that were in my stomach.

"Trin, are you okay?" I heard Kianna call out to me. "Oh my God, Trinity." She said as she held my hair while I continued to puke my insides up.

Finally, after ten minutes of dry heaving over the toilet, I stood up. "Are you okay?" Kianna asked me again, and I didn't know how to answer that. I was nowhere near okay. See, Onyx, after all these years, had me feeling the same as I did after all those years ago.

I rinsed my mouth before I answered her. "I-I'm good." I lied.

She gave me a look like she knew I was lying. "How long we've been knowing each other? You do know I know when you're lying right. Talk to me, tell me what's wrong."

Tears escaped my eyes as I shook my head. "I need to go home. I need to get out of here."

"Trinity, wait. Calm down. Please don't tell me after all these years you still have feelings for him. I mean, it's been what, more than ten years. Get over it already!" Kianna fussed.

My mouth fell open. I know Kianna can sometimes be rude, but, she knew more than anyone the pain I endured when Onyx broke my heart. "Really, Kianna?" Was all I could say. I don't know if her ass is too drunk that she doesn't realize what she's "I can't believe \\you acting like Onyx and I didn't have nothing real.”

“Really? Trinity, you were seventeen. Like, come on now get over him. Now, let’s go back there and finish our-”

I turned around and left out of the restroom before I cursed Kianna ass out and said some shit I will regret later.

I didn’t bother to turn around when I heard her call my name. I need to get out of here quick and fast. I walked over to the bar to pay my tab. I don’t have time going to jail over dining and ditching.

“Trinity, can I talk to for a minute?” I exhaled loudly and ignored him as I waited for the waiter to come back with my credit card. I swear if she doesn’t hurry up, I’m not tipping her! “Trinity, please, you owe me that much.”

My head snapped in direction so fast; I almost got whiplash. “Owe you? I don’t owe you shit!”

“Actually, you do!” He replied nonchalantly.

“I know you fuckin’ lying! I don’t owe you shit!” I yelled as I quickly snatched up my card and stormed away from the bar. The audacity for him to feel as if I owe him something.

I can feel the tears burning to escape my eyes, yet; I sucked them up. I cried many days and nights over Onyx. He was my first everything, and just when I was planning to spend the rest of my life with him, he was taken from me like a theft in the night.

I finally made it to my car, quickly got in, and let out a loud scream from the depths of my soul. Tears poured from my eyes as I began to relive my last moments with Onyx. I gave him the one thing in the world I can never get back.

A loud knock on my window caused me to jump. I looked and saw Onyx standing there. Exhaling loudly, I started my car.

“Trinity! Please! I just want ten minutes of your time.” The look of remorse on his face did something to me. I cursed myself for even caring about him.

I slowly exhaled and rolled down my window just enough for me to hear him. "What?" I snapped.

"Come on, Trinity, be serious for a minute."

I cut my eyes at him. "I am being serious." Reluctantly, I jumped out of the car and stood in front of him. I looked at the ground because I knew if I looked into his eyes, it would be over. "What do you have to say that's so damn important that you ruined my night out with my friend, huh? Don't you think you've ruined me enough?" I yelled. I didn't even realize that I was crying until he wiped the tear that rolled down my face.

He lifted my head so I can look at him. Just the warmth of his hand that rested against my face caused me to instantly calm down. "Damn, I didn't know I hurt you this bad, Poor bear." He spoke softly in my ear. The scent of his cologne danced around my nostrils. He wrapped his arms around me and held me tightly. "Damn, I've missed you, girl." I held my thighs together tightly. My body was betraying me. Being in his arms made me feel things I know I shouldn't. I inhaled deeply; being in his presence felt so familiar. I felt protected, loved, and cherished. Something I haven't felt with Aiden in a while.

"So, this is why you broke up with me, Damon? So, you can be with this fat ass bitch?" I quickly moved away from Onyx and came face to face with the enraged woman.

I eyed her up and down. I'm no hater and always give credit when due, and this woman is beautiful. However, she doesn't know me to be calling me out of my name. "Um… Hi, my name is Trinity, not bitch. It's nice to meet you, though." I said as I extended my hand out for her to shake, trying to lighten up the situation.

She looked at my hand like it had shit then turned her attention to Onyx. "So, is the bitch you broke up with me for? Huh? After I'm the one who held you down while you were in jail? ANSWER ME!" She screamed.

I chuckled to myself as I looked over at Onyx, he looked unbothered by her actions. Just like a man to not give a damn.

I shook my head and began to get into my car. "Trinity, wait!" He called out to me.

I scoffed and shook my head. "Nah, you're busy," I said, referring to the woman standing in front of him about to make a fool of herself. I knew the look in her eyes all too well. Gone behind a man.

I didn't bother waiting for him to reply. I quickly got into my car, started it, then pulled out of the parking lot. Leaving Onyx and his woman standing there to handle their business. One thing about me is I am no home wrecker, and plus, at the end of the day, I am an engaged woman, whose wedding is in six months.

I peeked in the rearview mirror and saw Onyx watching me as I drove away. Something about the way he looked at me sent shivers down my spine. Something tells me that this isn't going to be my last time seeing Onyx.

Love takes time

Michelle

I was trying my hardest to remain calm and think before I do something that I will regret. I stood in front of him, waiting for him to actually acknowledge me, which he has yet to do. He stood in the same spot I caught him hugging the bitch.

Whoever this bitch that he was hugged up with must be someone he cared for because here I am the woman who has held him down for the last four years. Yet, he basically said that he doesn't love me and never have. So, in other words, he used me.

Four years of my life that I put on hold for him when I could have been getting love from a man who actually loved me. And what pissed me off, even more, was the fact that he was still watching the bitch car as it drove away like I really wasn't standing here.

"Hello. You don't see me standing here?" I waved my hands in front of his face.

"Yeah but, I don't know why your here. When I wanted to talk you got up and walked away, well, that was after you threw your drink in my face. So, what is that saying you be saying when you on the phone with your friends? Oh yeah, keep that same energy." My mouth fell open wide as I watched him walk away.

"Damon! Damon! Don't just walk away from me!" I screamed at him. He stopped and turned to face me.

"Michelle, when you had the opportunity to talk to me, you

didn't. I wanted us to end this shit and still be friends but, you weren't trying to hear me. Now, all that shit you trying to say, I ain't trying to hear it."

"Do you love her?" Was the only thing I could say. After seeing how he was holding onto as if he never wanted to let her go, showed he cared for her more than me.

He chuckled as he ran his hand down his face. "Go home, Michelle."

"No, answer me! Come on, just be real. Do you love her or not?" He looked me dead in my eyes and just walked away from me, ignoring my questions.

Hurt and anger couldn't begin to describe the way I felt watching him just walk away from me. It was me who stood by his side for the last four years when he didn't have no one else. It was me that pushed him to do better on the inside so that when he comes home that he can be better in the real world. It was me, who went out and got a second job just to make sure he had money on his books, and he had a real home to come too when he was released.

After all that, he still chooses to say fuck me. He gives me this check of money; he assumed I wanted back and just leave. As if I am supposed to be okay with this? I'm not the least bit okay with his actions. The money isn't what I wanted. I wanted what was promised to me. I wanted the love he promised, the marriage, the kids. I want everything I know I deserved.

Damon owed me his heart, and I'm not going to stop until I get what I deserve and what I deserve is his heart. I'm not stopping until I get it.

Single player games

Onyx

I sat at my desk in deep thumbing through the child support papers. All I could do was shake my head. I didn't surprise me that Brooke sent me these paper before even letting me see my alleged daughter.

The last few days have been hell with Michelle blowing up my phone none stopped now, this.

Yes, I fucked with Brooke back in the day I can admit to that but, I don't recall fuckin' her raw. The only female I've ever hit raw is Trinity. Speaking of Trinity, I still can't believe that I saw her again. The day I went off to jail, I knew deep down there was a possibility that I was never going to see her again.

Just to see and touch her, let me know that she is the woman that is supposed to be in my life. I felt something deep inside of myself that I haven't felt in forever. Something that I couldn't explain but, I knew it came from seeing her.

When I first got locked up, I started to read the bible. One of the things I took from that what is supposed to be in your life will always come back to you. Seeing Trinity again, let me know that it's real.

I don't even know where to start by finding her again. Sitting at the expensive ass restaurant until she shows up again isn't an option. I'm not going to give up so quickly. I know Trinity is supposed to be with me, and I'm not going to stop looking for her. Until we meet again, I will focus back on what's important.

I turned attention back to the child support papers. I noticed there was an address at the top. I looked at the clock and saw that I had about two hours to kill before I opened the shop. I picked up my keys and headed out of the shop. Brooke got me fucked up if she thinks I'm going to just pay for a child I don't think is mine without seeing the child first.

~~~

I pulled up in front of Brooke's apartment complex. Taking in the surroundings, I should have known this is where she was going to end up in life. The projects. Growing up in the slums, I always wanted better out of life. I never wanted to be a product of my environment. My mama never cared about my brother or me, her only care was getting high the next day. Even though we had a roof over our head and food to eat, we didn't have the love from her. I made a promise to myself that I will never ever give my child the same up bring I had. I guess I can't say that about everyone.

I parked my car, got out, and headed towards her building before I could even make it to her door. I heard someone calling my name from behind me. I turned around to see Brooke standing there looking like a damn streetwalker.

Her weave was matted on top of her head, the dress she wore was short, barely covering her ass. All I could do was shake my head. I can't believe this is the type of woman that I might have a child with.

"Onyx, what are you doing here?"

I couldn't even answer her; I was too caught up in her appearance. Back in the day, Brooke was fine, slim thick about hundred and forty pounds, cute face, always kept herself up, and now, she looked like a strung-out dope fiend. She couldn't weigh any more than a hundred pounds soaking wet. I can only imagine what my daughter has been exposed too.
~~~

Damn, did I already claim the little girl as mine?

"Hello." She waved her dirty ass hand in my face. "You don't hear me talking to you?" I yelled, and I caught wind of something funky.

I took a step back and covered my nose. "Nah, I don't hear you but, I smell you loud and clear. When was the last time yo' ass took a bath?"

"What the fuck do you want!" She screamed.

I looked her up and down and still couldn't believe she looked like this. "I'm here to see my daughter claim I have."

Her eyes narrowed at me. "I'll see you in court, make sure you have my check ready." She said, trying to walk away but, I grabbed her hand, stopping her.

"Is that all she is to you a check?" I asked.

"Onyx, get the fuck out my face."

I followed behind Brooke until she reached her apartment. If she thought that she was getting rid of me any time soon, she was sadly mistaken. There is no way I'm leaving until I see the girl.

"So, you just go follow me?" She asked, and I ignored her. I watched closely as she unlocked the door. The second the door opened, a stench so horrible hit me directly in my face.

"What the fuck?" I mumbled to myself as I follow behind her into the apartment. Even though the apartment had a funky smell to it, it was semi-clean. I closed the door behind me and stood at the door. I didn't want to move any further into the apartment. By the stench there for sure had to be a dead body stash somewhere or some old ass funky underwear.

"Damiana, come here!" She yelled as she walked into her small kitchen area. Damn, she really named her after me.

For some reason, I couldn't keep my eyes off Brooke. I still can't believe after all these years that she has ended up like this. I never would have guessed it.

"Yes, ma'am." My eyes followed where the small sweet voice came from, and my heart stopped. "Yes, mama, you called me?" She spoke again, looking directly at Brooke. She never noticed me standing by the door. Brooke pointed over at me. When her eyes met mine, I knew right then and there that she is mine.

She shared the same features as my mama, and those big dark brown eyes and thick bushy eyebrows has me written all over them. Damn, I can't believe I really have a daughter. I know I shouldn't claim her before I get a test, but something deep down tells me that she is my daughter.

"You said you always you wanted to meet yo' daddy, there he goes." She pointed at me before she walked off towards the back of the apartment, leaving us alone. The shit really caught me off guard how she just left her daughter alone with me.

She hasn't seen me in over ten years, don't know nothing about me, I could be a damn killer, and yet she just leaves her daughter with me like its nothing. Some fuckin' mama she is. If the test comes back that she really is my daughter, the first thing I'm going to do is file for custody because Brooke ass is definitely unfit.

I mean here it is the early morning, Damiana isn't in school, and Brooke left her alone at home for God knows how long. Yeah, her ass is definitely unfit to be a mother to any child that came out my nut sack.

"Hello, my name is Damon. What is your name?" I asked as I walked closer to her.

She narrowed her eyes at me, then looked back at where Brooke walked off to with a worried look on her face. I cursed Brooke's ass for putting me in this predicament. You would think her ass would want to be here to have this conversation with Damiana. It's not liked her ass is a baby; she old enough to understand, which also means she going to have questions that I feel both Brooke and I need to answer.

"Um.. are you really my dad?" She asked, ignoring my question. Her question caught me off guard. If I say yes and she happens to not be my daughter, then what am I supposed to say? It's clear that Brooke doesn't give a fuck either way. Quickly shaking those thoughts out my head, I replied, "Yes, I am your dad." When the results come in, I will cross that bridge when the time comes. Right, now the only thing that matters is my beautiful daughter.

A wide smile spread across her beautiful face before she jumped into my arms, hugging me tightly.

"Daddy!" She cheered.

A warm feeling came over me; I don't know how to describe it because it's something I never felt before. Hold her in my arms made something inside of me want to do everything in my power to protect her.

"Daddy, I'm hungry. I haven't eaten since lunch yesterday."

I instantly became pissed. "Why haven't you eaten?" She shrugged her shoulder.

I instantly became pissed all over again. I made my way back to where I saw Brooke walk off to. I didn't bother knocking on the door; I busted into the room only for my worst fears to be confirmed.

Brooke was taking a pull from a crack pipe. Crack!

Before I realize what, I had my hands wrapped around her neck, choking the fuck out of her. "Bitch, is you dumb? Yo' ass smoking that shit while yo' fuckin' daughter in here!" I yelled in her face.

She was scratching my hands, trying to get me to let her go. "Onyx-" She tried to speak.

"Shut the fuck up! I'm taking my fuckin' daughter with me, and the next time I see you, you better have your shit together. Or when it's time to go to court, I'ma let the judge know how you rather suck on a glass dick than be a fucking mother!" I threw her to the floor then turned to leave out of the room.

Brooke was on the floor crying and gasping for air.

I grabbed Damiana's hand and walked out of the apartment. I know if I don't get away from Brooke's ass, I might just end up killing her for real.

"Daddy, where are we going?" I couldn't even answer her because I don't know the first thing about taking care of a child. Against better judgement, I pulled out my phone and called the only person; I know that will help me.

"Hello." She answered.

"Michelle, I need you."

Find our love again

Aiden

"So, Aiden, are you ready to share to Trinity about what happened to you in the past that makes you lash out the way you do?"

I groaned to myself. When I told Trinity that I would seek therapy, I was just saying whatever I could to keep her. I didn't think she really wanted me to go through with this shit.

"Aiden? We are waiting." I cut my eyes at my therapist.

I exhaled loudly and turned to face Trinity. I don't know what I was about to say because I didn't have any childhood trauma that makes me do what I do. If Trinity acted like my damn woman, I wouldn't have to put my hands on her.

Growing up, I watched my mama be submissive to my dad. When my dad told my mama something, she listened. My dad always taught us that the man is the head of the household. When Trinity and I get married, I'm going to stress that OBEY in is our vows because when she says her vows, I'm going to hold her to that. Trinity will obey me as her husband, or she is going to suffer at my hands.

"Baby." I grabbed her hands and stared into her eyes. "You are my world, and I never want to do anything to hurt you. Growing up, I watched my dad be the head of the household. He worked, and my mama stayed home and cared for my brothers and myself. When he would tell her something, she would listen to him.

There was this one time she disagreed with him, and he slapped her. After that, she never disagreed with him ever again."

"That was back then. This is a whole different era. If you haven't noticed, women aren't as dependent on men nowadays."

"I understand that but, the bible says a woman is to be submissive to her husband." I reminded her.

"Keyword husband, Aiden. Something you aren't yet. Something you won't be if you continue to have this mindset." She snapped back. I bit back from commenting on what she just said. I could feel my face burning with anger. I am trying my hardest to keep calm, but every time Trinity opened her mouth, I became more and more pissed.

"Trinity-" I started but, she cut me off. Something she has been getting more comfortable doing.

"No. Listen. I know you was raised in a very traditional household, and I understand why your mind is the way it is, but you cannot turn me into your mama. I am not a homemaker who will depend on her husband for everything. I'm not saying that it didn't work for your parents. I'm just saying it won't work for us."

"How do you know that?" I asked.

"For one, I am not your mama. Two, I have my own career, money, and self-respect. I don't need a man. A man is simply an option."

I lost my shit. "What the fuck are you saying Trinity because all I'm getting is this whack as I AM EVERY WOMAN bullshit." All the pep-talking I gave myself went out the window.

"Aiden, I'm going to have to ask you to calm down. The purpose of her being is for you and her to both express yourselves without the other person getting upset or feeling attacked."

"How am I supposed to feel then?" I snapped. How the fuck did, she expect me to feel when my own woman is sitting here telling me she doesn't need me. I don't know whether my ego was wounded or the fact that Trinity, for some odd reason, feels she can speak for herself now. Hell, when we first met, I couldn't get her to think for herself.

Throughout the rest of the meeting, I just sat there and allowed the both of them to tell me what is wrong with me. I responded by nodding and grunting. When our time was up, I damn near ran out of the office. I was fuming, and at this point, if we don't get out of here, I am going to lose my shit!

"Wow, I feel so much better. Aiden, thank you for asking me to come to therapy with you. I really feel that this is just what we need in order for us to have a successful marriage. Don't you think?"

I cut my eyes over at her. The way her eyes light up as she as she looked over at me. Just the fact she was so happy was like lightning fueled added onto the burning fire that was burning inside of me. "You enjoy that, didn't you?" I asked because I know there was no hell that she ws

"Of course, I did. Didn't you?" I didn't reply. I put my attention back onto the road and allowed the conversation to die down. The only sounds that could be heard in the car is the low jazz as we both were left to deal with our own thoughts.

Thirty minutes later, I pulled into our driveway. The minute I put the car in park Trinity turned to face me.

"Aiden, I know going through therapy isn't easy for you. However, I feel like this is the right step we need to take to make our future strong." She kissed my cheek then jumped her ass out the car.

I watched as she walked off towards the front door and let exhaled loudly. Even though I didn't learn shit at the therapy session. I did take note that Trinity is starting to become into herself. If I keep putting my hands on her, then she will really leave my ass this time, and there won't be shit that I can do to make her stay.

My phone ringing pulled me from my thoughts. As soon as I saw the name scroll across the screen, I instantly became irritated.

"What!" I answered.

"Well, hello to you too."

"What the fuck you are calling me for, I'm not in the mood for none of your bullshit right now, Kianna."

"The first is right around the corner I'm just calling making sure you have my money ready." I let out a deep sigh. This shit with Kianna has been going on for far too long. I'm going to have to tell Trinity the truth about this situation between Kianna and I because I can't continue to allow this trick to suck me dry of all my damn money.

"I'm going to tell Trinity about us." I blurted.

The line went quiet then beeped twice, indicating that she hung up.

I have to figure out how to right, my wrongs with Kianna. Before it's all too late and I lose what's important. Trinity.

It's never too late

Trinity

"Trin, are you sure that's the vail you want?" I heard my mama ask me but, I was too caught up in the mirror looking at my reflection in my wedding dress. Today is my final dress fitting. I'm here with my mama, Kianna, and my other bride's maids. They were all having a good time drinking wine; meanwhile, I was conflicted with my feelings about this entire wedding.

Running my hands down my beautiful, elegant mermaid style gown. I picked this dress almost a year and a half ago. I remember being so excited when I first picked this dress.

Aiden told me there was no limit when it came to the wedding. So, I picked a five thousand dollar without thinking. You couldn't tell me nothing when I bought it. Now, as I look at myself in it, I realize that I don't even want this dress. I don't know if I even want this wedding.

After attending therapy with Aiden, I thought things were going to get better but, I wrong. He hasn't laid a hand on me, but that didn't stop the verbal abuse. I have lost count of how many times he has called me out of my name or threatened to beat me.

When I tried to talk to him about the exercises that the therapist gave us, he didn't want to hear that shit. All he would do is scream and break shit. Then the next day it's as if nothing has happened. I'm real life living Dr. Jekyll and Mr. Hyde. I'm mentally tired of all the bullshit.

I'm tired of walking on eggshells in my own home. I'm scared of having to think about what not to say that will set him off. I'm just tired of pretending that I'm happy when in reality, I'm miserable.

"Trin, honey, are you okay? Why are you crying?"   I didn't even realize that I was crying.

I quickly wiped my face and walked back to my dressing room. More tears fell as I tried my hardest to get myself together. Everything wasn't going how I planned them, and honestly, I'm starting to feel like my relationship with Aiden is really over. Yet, how do I explain that to him and our family? So much money has already been invested into this wedding from both of our parents.

"Trin baby, let mama in." My mama called from the outside of the door. I wiped the rest of my tears before I opened up the door for her.

Yes, ma'am."

She rubbed her hand down my face like she used to when I was a little girl. "What is wrong with you? Today is supposed to be a happy day, yet here you're crying. I didn't go through fourteen hours of labor, forty-eight hours of no food, and eight weeks without sex for you to be unhappy." She said, causing me to laugh.

"You always say that." I laughed.

"I'm going to keep saying it because I know that I will put a smile on your face each time. Now, tell mama what's wrong. Why are you crying? Is it Aiden?"

I let out a deep sigh and nodded. "Mama, I don't think I want to go through with this wedding," I confessed.

I held my breath as I waited for her to curse me out about the money that was already spent and the time we put into this wedding.

"Well, if this is how you feel, then I suggest you go home and have this talk to Aiden. Meanwhile, I'll begin the cancellations." She replied as she pulled out her phone.

"Ma' wait," I said, snatching her phone away from her. "Are you not go try to talk me out of it?"

She gave me a blank stare. "For what? If you feel like this, who am I to talk you out of it?"

I nodded as I handed her phone back, "You're right. But the wedding is three months away."

She shrugged. "I know I am, and plus if I remember correctly, I told you not to go back to him in the first place."

"I know mama but, you and daddy were hell-bent on me being married so-"

"So, you thought we wanted you to settle with a woman beater?" I nodded as more tears fell from my eyes. My parents are one of the reasons why I stayed with Aiden for this long. They had it in their mind that Aiden was the best thing for me, even after I told them otherwise. It took him to beat my ass for them to see that Aiden isn't as perfect as they thought. "Look, Trinity, I know me, and your daddy wanted you to get married off but, never in a million years did we want you to marry someone who didn't love you the same as we do. Being married isn't everything. I just want you to have someone to love you for you, that's all." She stated before pulling me into a tight hug.

No more words were said as I let out all the emotions that I've been holding in the last few weeks. I don't know how well this conversation with Aiden is going to go but, it's time that I be true to myself.

~ ~ ~

Pulling into the driveway of the house I shared with Aiden; I cringed at the thought of going into the house knowing Aiden was already in there. I slowly got out of my car and made my way to the front door.

I've been thinking about what to say to Aiden since we left the dress shop. Kianna tried to get me to go home with her, but I refused. I can't keep putting off the much-needed conversation. Nervous doesn't describe the way I feel as I enter the house. I placed my purse and keys onto the table that we kept next to the front door.

"Trin, is that you?" Aiden called out. "I'm in the kitchen."

I slowly counted from ten as I made my way to the kitchen. I needed to make sure I was calm in order for me to do this. With each step, I took my stomach felt like it was in knots.

My mouth fell open as soon as I entered the kitchen. Aiden stood next to the table that was cover in a red tablecloth, with a nice candle lit dinner. Rose petals covered the kitchen floor. My eyes went from Aiden to the table.

"What is all this?" I asked, confused. Aiden has never done anything romantic like this before.

"Well." He started as he walked closer to me. "I feel like this is the least I can do after how I've been acting lately." He pulled me into his arms and kissed my lips softly.

I pulled away from him and stared into his brown eyes. As much as I appreciate him doing all this for me but, I'm sad to say that this is all too late.

"Aiden, we need to talk."

"Yes, we do, and we will once we sit down." He grabbed my hand and pulled me towards the table.

My heart was beating so hard; it felt like it was going to burst out of my chest. At this moment, if I don't break up with Aiden, I know I will never do it. It's either now, or never. "Wait," I said as I pulled my hand away from him. "We need to talk about this now."

He gave me a blank stare. "What is so important-"

"I think we need to break up." I blurted out. The shock expression on Aiden's face didn't go unnoticed. "These last few weeks have been hard, and after today, after trying on my wedding dress for the final fitting, that's when I knew that I couldn't do this anymore. I love you Aiden I do. However, it is time that I start to love myself." I expressed.

Silence fell between us. The look on Aiden's face was unreadable. I didn't expect for him to react this way. Maybe he is just in shock, or maybe he wanted out of this relationship just as I did.

I cleared my throat after waiting ten minutes in silence. "Um... I'm going to start packing my stuff." I slowly slipped my engagement ring off my finger and laid it onto the kitchen counter. My eyes met his; the blank expression still covered his face.

I slowly turned and made my way out of the kitchen. As I made my way towards the stairs, it felt like everything was lifted from my shoulders. My heart does hurt because when Aiden asked me to marry him never in a million years did, I think we would end like this.

Aiden being the first guy I fell in love with after Onyx he changed something in me. He taught me how to love and be loved again. I dreamed that we were going to get married, have children, that weeklong vacations, and just be happy. I thought Aiden was going to my happily ever after; I guess I was wrong.

I began walking up the stairs when I heard Aiden call my name. I turned around and was met with a hard punch right in my face, sending me crashing to the floor. The sound of something cracking let me know that he broke my nose.

"Trinity, I have invested too much time and money into you. There is no way and hell that I'm going to let you think that you just going to get up and walk away from me. We not over until I saw we are."

I had to blink twice to make sure I wasn't dreaming. My eyes met his, and for the first time in our relationship, I saw the real Aiden staring back at me. The damn devil.

I opened my mouth to speak, "Don't do this." I begged him. "Can't you see that we both are unhappy?"

He scoffed. "Who said I was unhappy?"

I gave him a side-eye. "You did!" I yelled. "Every time you put your hands on me, yell at me, and tell me just the way you treat me!"

"How do I treat you, Trin? Huh? Please tell me?"

I opened my mouth to speak but thought against it. I know where Aiden is going with this conversation. I'm not about to allow him to bait me into this shit only for him to try to put his hands on me again.

"Aiden, please, let me go to the hospital. I think my nose is broken." I told him, trying to change the subject.

He shook his head and reached out to me. "Come on; I'll fix you up."

"What?" I asked, confused. "Did you not hear me? I said I think my nose is broken, which means I need to the fucking hospital!"

He chuckled. "See, that's why I keep putting my hands on you." I quickly moved to get away from Aiden's grasp. "Trinity, I'm going to say this one last time; We aren't over until I say it's over." Each word he spoke sent a chill down my spine. I can hear the seriousness and hate in his tone. I knew that what he was telling was the truth.

Now, not only do I fear Aiden even more now. I also fear for my life. Just when I thought my happiness was in my reach, it was snatched away from me. There has to be some other way that I can get out of this relationship.

Aiden moved closer to me and pulled me up from the floor by my shirt. He pulled me close to his face and gazed into my eyes. My heart was beating so fast it felt like it was going to burst out of my chest. I don't know what to expect any more when it comes to Aiden.

"You know you're about to be my wife, right?" He licked his lips as he eyed me up and down.

I knew the look in Aiden's eyes. My stomach cringed at the thought of what he might expected from me. I hope he doesn't expect me to have sex with him after he hit me.

"Yes," I responded, trying to figure out where he was going with this.

"And I wife takes care of her husband's needs, right?"

Just like I thought, he wants to have sex. My eyes fell to the bulge in his pants. My mouth became watery like I was going to throw up. "I-I'm not in the mood. My nose hurts really bad." I whispered. I hoped by telling him that he would understand.

As if I hadn't said anything, Aiden began to unbutton the pants I had on. "Aiden don't. Please no-"

Whap!

I fell onto the stairs sobbing uncontrollably. It was as if everything began to move in slow motion. Aiden snatched my pants off and entered me roughly. I cried out in pain because I was not ready.

"Shut the fuck up!" He growled as he roughly pumped in and out of me. He showed me no mercy, not that I expected him to.

I held in my cries because I know if I make another sound, Aiden might hit me again. His paced quickened, and his strokes became short. His loud grunts let me know that he was about to cum.

Aiden pulled out of me and began to nut all over me. My hair, my mouth, my eyes, and face. Tears fell from my eyes; I had never in my life experienced something so degrading before. I held my sobs in as reality set in.

Aiden's calm, he loves me so much, but there is no way he can love me when he does the things he does to me, IS doing to me. I don't know what I'm going to have to do to get out of this toxic relationship, but, I have to go before I end up dead.

Are you that somebody?

Michelle

I moved around the kitchen quickly as I tried to hurry and fix breakfast before Damon and Damiana came downstairs. It's only been three days since he called and told me he needed me. I knew he would come back to me; I was just surprised that he didn't come alone.

When I opened my door, I was shocked to see a girl version of Damon. At first, I wanted to slam the door in his face and say fuck him the same way he did me like he did that night. However, the stress and worry that covered Damon's face made me give in. He knew there was no way I can resist him.

"Good morning Ms. Michelle." Damiana greeted me as she walked into the kitchen.

"Good morning Damiana your breakfast is on the table go head and eat so I can take you to school."

"Yes, ma'am." She replied.

I was very shocked to learn that Damiana is a well-mannered, I mean considering how Damon explain to me her living situation with her mama. Speaking of her mama, it's been three damn days, and not once had she asked if she could call her mama or ask when she was going home. That right there says a lot about how her relationship with her mama is.

Especially when the last few days she has been clinging onto me.

I can see that she wants a woman to look up to. It's just sad that she can't get it from the woman she calls mama. Maybe that's why we get along so well.

My relationship with my own mama is nonexistent because of the choices I've made in the past. However, our relationship has always been strained. My mama hated me and never wanted to be bothered with me. Meanwhile, all I wanted was my mama.

"Good morning, ladies." Greeted me with a kiss on the cheek, pulling me from my thoughts.

I watched him go sit next to Damiana and kissed her on the cheek as well. I'm still in shock that my man has a daughter. I always thought that I was going to give him his first child but, that okay. As long as I'm able to give me the rest of his children.

I watched as they both laughed and played over breakfast. It warmed my heart to watch how Damon has taken on this parenting role. Those two have been as thick as thieves since they have gotten here.

Leaving them to enjoy their breakfast, I left out of the kitchen to get ready for work. I gathered the clothes I'm wearing for today and headed towards the bathroom. I turned the shower on and began to reflect on the conversation Damon and I had last night.

~~~

The warm water felt wonderful on my sore, aching bones. Who knew that shopping for a little girl could be so stressful? I love me some good retail therapy but, shopping for a ten-year-old with her own taste has been exhausted. After going to six different stores, all I want to do right now is get a bottle of wine and watch some ratchet Tv.

A knock on the door got my attention. "Come in," I called out.

The door opened, and Damon walked in with a bottle of red wine as if he could read my mind. "Hey."
~~~

"Hey, you," I replied. As I watched him pour me a glass of wine.

"Here you go." He handed me the wine, and I wasted no time downing the first glass. I'm not the sipping type of wine drinker. "Well, I take it that today was stressful?" He chuckled.

I handed him back the glass and laughed. "Very. Your daughter is very picky."

He chuckled, showing off his nice smile and white teeth. "She enjoyed herself with you, and she loves everything." He paused. "Thank you, Michelle. I honestly didn't know what I was thinking when I took her from her mama. All I knew was that I couldn't have her living in that type of situation."

"Why didn't you tell me you had a daughter?"

"Hell, I just found out about her myself. When Brooke first called me about her, I thought she was lying because I knew, well, I thought that I wrapped up when I was fucking with her. It wasn't until I laid eyes on Damiana that I knew in my heart that she was, in fact, my daughter." I saw the truth in his eyes as he spoke.

I pondered on the question I've been wanting to ask him since he called me. My feelings for him haven't changed since the last time we saw each other. Even after I saw him hugged up with that woman, even after he walked away from me as if I didn't mean anything to him. My love for him the reason why I answered the phone when he called. I love Damon, and I'm willing to do whatever that he needs me to do. However, I just don't know if I should.

The last time Damon and I was together, he expressed that he didn't share the same feelings as I thought he did about me. After the four years, I spent going back and forth to the jailhouse, writing him, and supporting him financially. I thought we had built something while he was locked down. I try to tell myself that it wasn't just jail talk, and I really do mean something to him. Yet, I can't bring myself to acknowledge that

Damon's words are true. I'm not dumb by a long shot, and I'm not crazy.

Deep down, I feel like he doesn't love me, yet he probably does feels obligated to me. I don't want to be getting emotionally attached to his daughter, only for him to take her away from me. I'm torn in what to do from this point.

One, I can play dumb and act as if everything is okay and go on like I don't know the truth. Two, I can ask him what our relationship status is and disrupted the 'peace' we have at the moment.

I'm a firm believer that certain people are put in your life for a reason, and in due time God will reveal their purpose.

After finishing getting myself together for the day, I made my way back into the kitchen only to find it empty.

"Damon!" I yelled but got no answer. I walked to the front of the house, looked out of the window, and saw that his car was gone. He didn't even say bye.

I pulled out my phone and dialed his number. The phone ring twice before it went to voicemail. I tried it two more times only to get the same result, nothing.

I let out a deep sigh, a million things began to run through my head. Did I do something wrong? Is he ever coming back? Did I do something wrong with Damiana? Does she not like me?

Just when I thought I was about to have a mental break down, my phone began to ring. Damon's number flashed across the screen. I smile slowly formed on my face. My ass was sitting here overthinking when he probably busy.

I swiped left answering. "Hey, bae-" My words were cut off when I heard Damon's voice talking to someone else. "Damon," I called out again. When he didn't respond, I knew he had accidentally called me.

Just as I was about to end the call, I heard a woman's voice in the background. My body instantly froze. I've heard that voice before, the voice of the woman belonged to the same woman that I saw Damon hugged up with.

My heart instantly dropped into the pit of my stomach. Just when I thought things between Damon and I was getting better here, she comes in messing shit up. I don't know or care who this woman is; she is in for rude awaken if she thinks that she is about to take Damon away from me.

I told him when he was behind those walls that it's going to be us, and I meant just that.

*You and I will always have
unfinished business. . .*

Onyx

I hated to leave the house while Michelle was in the shower but, Tanz called and said there was an emergency at the shop. I know she is going to feel some type of way because I left without saying bye. These last couple of days, she has been really helpful when it came to my daughter.

She came right in and began to care for Damiana as if she was her own child. The shit kinda fuck me up for a minute because I was expecting Michelle to be so open to me helping me after shit ended between us the other night.

I've been trying to see where her mind is because, I want her to know even though, I asked her for help my decision about our relationship. I want us to be friends, nothing more.

"Daddy, it's my turn to bring snacks to class this week. I really want to bring them this time. Mama never cared to bring them, and everyone in my class would always make fun of me. Calling me poor and dirty." The sadness I heard in my baby girl's voice pissed me off. Her beautiful smile was turned into a frown, and that's when I really notice that she and I share a lot of similarities.

I gripped the stirring wheel tighter, trying to hold my tongue. If I didn't like Brooke already, this shit just added to it. I don't know what type of fuck shit her ass was on but, if I have any say so, Damiana will never go back with her.

"Okay, baby girl, we go get you some snacks and some good snacks too. So that all your classmates can be jealous." I told her. Damiana frown turned back into that bright smile warmed my heart. This daddy shit is new to me but, I'll do anything to keep that smile on her face.

Whatever is going on at the shop can wait because right now, the only thing that is important is being the parent my daughter deserves. Man, the shit still feels unreal. If someone would have told me six months ago that I was going to be a father, I probably would have cursed them out. I always wanted kids, but I figure it would happen once I got married. I guess God has his own timing.

Looking around, I noticed a Walgreens and quickly pulled into the parking lot. "Come on, let get those snacks for your class. We have to hurry, don't want you to be late."

Ten minutes and forty dollars later, we walked out the door with three bags full of snacks. Damiana ran off and got into the car. She was so excited about going to school now that she had the snacks for her class.

I was too busy texting Tanz back that I never noticed the person walking in front of me until it was too late, and we both bumped into each other hard.

"My bad. Excuse me." I reached out to help her up. Something about her was very familiar; I just couldn't put my finger on where I knew her from. Her long hair and large shades cover a majority of her face for me to really see her face.

"Ouch! Watch where you going-" Her words trailed off, and that's when I knew exactly who she is.

"Trinity."

"Onyx."

We both said in unison. My heartbeat increased, seeing her

standing in front of me.

Trinity has been the only woman in my life that can make me feel like a female on the inside. When we were together years ago, I tried to fight the hold she had on me. I just couldn't admit that a young ass girl had me feeling all mushy on the inside. I tried talking even fuckin' other females while I was with Trinity and none of those females made me feel the way she did. Hell, women twice her age still couldn't make me feel the same as she did. But, by the time I finally admit to myself that I loved her just as much as she loved me, I was locked up.

This is my first time seeing her since the night at the restaurant, and Trinity is different. Nothing physically that I could notice right away but, the tone of her voice as she spoke, and her body language. Something was up with her. The Trinity I knew ten years ago had the biggest brightest smile that could light up the entire sky. Yet, the Trinity in front of me wasn't the same. Maybe life for her has been as well as I thought.

She must have been just as shock to see me as I saw her. Her mouth was slightly hung opened. Dallas isn't a small city, so I'm going to take this as a sign that Trinity and I meeting today isn't a coincidence. "Hey, how are you?" I asked her to break the silence between us.

Her head dropped down. "Excuse me." She tried to walk past me, ignoring my question. The fact that she called herself ignoring me triggered something in me, and before I realized what I was doing, I snatched her by her arm, pulling her into my body.

"What is wrong with you?" I hissed. She tried to snatch her arm away from me but, my grip was too tight. "Stop fighting me and talk to me."

"Onyx please, this isn't the right time." I could hear the desperation in her voice. It was a silent plea for help. Without thinking, I snatched the shades off her face, and all the wind was knocked out of my throat when I saw what she was hiding.

Her beautiful face was covered in bruises, both of her eyes were black damn near swollen shut, I'm surprised that she could even see, and her sexy plumped lips were bussed. Seeing her like this caused me to see nothing but red.

What type of nigga is she fucking with that put his hands on her like this? I don't care what she did; no woman ever deserved to be beaten like this.

"Onyx please I need to go-"

"Who did this to you?" I asked, cutting her off.

"Please I need to-"

"WHO THE FUCK DID THIS TO YOU TRINITY?"

I was not about to allow her to continue to brush me off like that like the shit was normal. She opened her mouth to speak, but nothing came out. She collapsed into my arms and cried.

All I could do was wrap my arms around her and hold her tightly as she cried into my chest. The only thing I could think about since the last time I saw her was her being in my arms. I closed my eyes and inhaled her sweet scent.

My moment of happiness was snatched from me when I heard Damiana's voice. "Daddy, who is she?" I was so wrapped up in Trinity I forgot about Damiana. I opened my mouth to reply but, Trinity cut me off.

"Daddy?" She looked at Damiana and then back at me. "Onyx, how old is she?" I saw the look of confusion on her face.

Before I can respond, Damiana answered for me. "I'm ten."

I cursed on the inside because I already know that Trinity was putting two and two together. Yes, I was fucking around with different females while I was dealing with Trinity but, it's not what I'm sure she thinks it was. I need her to allow me to explain to her my reasons behind it.

"Trinity, look before you start trying to put two and two together let me explain."

She pulled away from me and scoffed. "No, there is no need to explain. Her age says it all; I just hate that. . ." She paused. I knew she was hurt but, at the end of the day my daughter is here and there is nothing that can change that. "I just hate that I thought you were different."

"Trinity, hear me out," I begged her.

"No, I don't to hear it. I have to go. Have a good day." She pushes passed me. My mind was going a mile a minute. I know if I allow Trinity to leave, there can be a possibly that I could never see her again. I quickly snatched her arm and pulled her hard into my body. "What the-"

"Get the fuck in the car now! Yo' ass ain't running away from me no more. We have a lot of shit to discuss." I growled in her ear. My grip around her arm was tight, letting her know I was serious.

She narrowed her eyes at me. "We have nothing to talk about!" She fired back.

A smile crept across my face seeing feisty Trinity slowly starting to resurface.

"Pooh bear, you and I will always have something to talk about." Her eyes softened when she realized I called her by the nickname I'd given her.

"Onyx, please."

"Nah, I'm not trying to hear that. Get. In. The. Car." I told her as I pointed to my car. She looked at me for a minute like I was going to change my mind before she stomped off towards my car.

Watching her getting into my car, I let out a sigh of relief. The hard part of getting her to agree to go with me was over. I've been waiting for this moment since the night at the restaurant.

I don't care about her little attitude; she needs to realize that we will always have unfinished business. Starting with what fuck nigga did that shit to her fuckin' face.

I don't know what I feel anymore. . .

Trinity

How does a trip to the pharmacy end up like this?

Sitting in the back seat of Onyx's car, trying to convince myself that I was doing the right thing by being here. We did have unfinished business to tend to. Then every time I said it, I realized just how dumb I sound. Here I am in the car of my first love, who I just learned was basically living a double life when we were together. I tried to convince myself that it was ten years ago, and it didn't matter anymore. However, the fact of the matter is he still cheated. Something I thought he would never do to me. I guess I was wrong.

However, all that shouldn't even matter because I am about to be a married woman is less than ninety days. Just thinking about marrying Aiden made me cringe. The last couple of days with him have been pure hell. The days of beatings. Three days of being yelled at. Three days of being raped. Just thinking about the events that transpired over the last three days bought tears to my eyes.

I'm so glad that Aiden had to go to work today because I don't know how much more I could take of his abuse. Both of my eyes are black and purple, my lip is busted, and it felt like my nose was broken. This morning when I sat in front of the mirror, all I could do was cry. I allowed myself to become this woman who I didn't even recognize. I had to call off from work for a few weeks because there is no way that I could return to work with my face like this. I allowed a man to have so much control over me that I didn't know which way to turn.

I was too embarrassed to even call my parents because I didn't want to hear the 'I told you so' and calling Kianna was out the question. Lately, she has been distant, and I blamed it on the fact that I went back to Aiden after she told me not to. I was alone and confused.

Leaving Aiden has been on my mind heavy, yet after what I endured over the last three days. I don't know if I would ever be able to do it. I don't know if I can ever be with another man after the way Aiden treated me.

"Trinity, did you hear me?" Onyx's deep voice snapped me from my thoughts.

"What?" I snapped.

"I said we are here. Calm down, damn!" He hissed then got out of the car.

I looked out the window and noticed that we were sitting outside of a beautiful house. The light brown home was newly built, just the rest of the block. The landscape was perfect, and it was a different type of environment than what I know Onyx is used too.

My car door opened, and Onyx reached his hand out to me. "Come on, man, let's go inside and talk."

I narrowed my eyes at him. "Talk? What do we need to talk about, Onyx? What we had has come and gon-" Before I could even finish my sentence, Onyx snatched me out of the car. I tried my hardest to fight the hold he had on me, but it was pointless. He was too damn strong for me. "Unhand me!" I shouted. "I am not going into that woman's house with you! I am not a home-wrecker!"

"Shut the hell up! I do have fuckin' neighbors' crazy ass! Last time I checked, I owned this house." He growled at me.

I looked at the house then back at him, confused. This couldn't be his house, right? "T-This is your house?"

He narrowed his eyes at me. "Yeah, this is my house. What you trying to say, huh? I can't afford no shit like this?" He snapped back, getting defensive.

"Um… I mean… well you did just get out of jail. How can you afford this?" As soon as those words came out my mouth, I regretted them. I knew it would make me sound stuck up, but that wasn't how I was trying to come off. "Onyx wait, I didn't mean-"

"Wow, Trinity. Since when you become so damn judgmental?"

I could sense the hurt in his voice. The last thing I wanted to do was come off like that. I opened my mouth to speak, but quickly thought against it. I don't need to say nothing else. The last thing I need is for Onyx to take his anger out on me the same way that Aiden did. I don't know if my body and my soul can take it.

Onyx grip on my arm loosened before he pulled me into the direction of the front door. I stayed quiet as we enter the house. The moment I stepped inside the house, my breath was taken away by the design of the house. I mean, the outside was nice but, it didn't do the inside no justice. The gold, white, and hunter green décor was nice. I noticed that he didn't have much furniture. He had the basics which every home is supposed to have. Guilt began to set in when I realized that I judged this man without even knowing him fully. I mean, yes, I know him but, I do not know the man that Onyx has become. All I know is the younger Onyx. The Onyx that I fell in love with. The Onyx that broke me.

I slowly pulled away from him. "I'm sorry."

"Don't be." He replied. I still can sense his attitude, but I decided not to speak on it. "Are you hungry?" He asked, and I shook my head no. As sweet as I know, he's trying to be or whatever. Eating has been the last thing on my mind these last few days. I really need to see about getting back to my car and get what I actually went to Walgreens for.

After about ten or fifteen minutes of just standing there, staring at each other. I decided to speak up first. "Are you going to talk? I mean, I do have something to do."

Onyx turned to face me. "Yeah, as soon as you start explaining about that." He said, pointing to my face.

I shook my head. The last thing I want to do is talk about my face. Onyx will never understand, and I'm not in the mood to be judged. "There's nothing to explain. So, can you take me back to my car."

"Nah, I can't. I'm not going to let you go back to whatever nigga is putting his hands on you. So, I suggest you get comfortable." He began to walk off like his word actually meant something to me.

I rushed behind him. "Wait a damn minute. You don't run nothing over here!" I shouted at him.

"Actually, I do. This is my house, or have you forgotten?" He smirked, showing off that one dimple that used to make me weak in the knees.

Clearing my throat, I ran my hands through my tangled hair. Staring at him right now, I was getting nervous. Onyx always had a way of making me feel like I am the only girl in the world when he looks at me. "Look, Onyx say what you have to say because I have to go back to the store, I mean you just took me away-"

"Tell me what you need, and I'll go get it." He replied, cutting me off. Something I've noticed he's done a lot since he bought me here.

"No, Onyx." I paused and exhaled. I've had enough stress, and at this point, I can deal with nothing else. I just broke down crying in the middle of the living room. I fell to my knees and just cried.

I cried for everything that I've endured. My sobs were so loud it caused my ears to ring.

"Damn, Pooh bear." I heard Onyx say but, I couldn't even speak. My entire soul was broken. I have never in my left felt the way I have at this moment. My life with Aiden is not what I expected it to be. When Aiden came into my life, I'd haven't been with a man in a long time. I thought that I would never find love again. Then when Aiden came into my life, it was like a breath of fresh air, fast forward to now he is the devil in disguise. I don't know if I would ever love Aiden the way I used too.

"Shhhh, stop all that crying." Onyx swooped me up in his arms and carried me off towards the back of the house.

I wanted to protest but, being in his arms made me feel safer than I have in months. I know I shouldn't feel this way with him because at the end of the day this man who I loved a long time ago, isn't the man who I thought he was.

Onyx laid me down in the middle of his big bed and got into the bed with facing me. "I don't know what you've been going through; I just want you to know that I am here for you."

My only focus right now is going to be getting back to my old self. Getting back to Trinity. Onyx voice was soothing, even though I don't know what the hell he's talking about. The last thing I heard before my eyes drifted closed was him promising to never leave my side. He sounded so sincere; at the same time, I can't just allow myself to fall victim to another man's lies.

~~~

The aroma of something tasty danced around my nostrils. My eyes fluttered open to see Onyx standing at the end of the bed, holding a tray with a bag of food from Popeyes.

I chuckled, "Still can't cook, huh?"

"Man, the stuff I can cook, you not going to eat. Come on, get up; you've been sleep for eight hours."

I jumped out the bed and began to search for my stuff. "Oh my,
~~~

Onyx, I have to go." I turned and saw him still standing in the same spot. "Hello!" I waved in his face. "You didn't hear me? Where is my stuff I need to go?" I shouted. I began to get angry because I didn't plan on staying here thing long. I know Aiden is at home, probably going ape shit crazy because I am not there. The last thing I want is to deal with the wrath of Aiden.

"Sit down, Trinity."

"No Onyx I need to go-"

"I SAID, SIT DOWN!" He demanded.

Doing as I was told, I sat down on the edge of the bed. The tone of his voice did something to me. I was both turned on and pissed off.

He walked over to me and sat the tray down on the bed. "Eat the food, and then when you're ready, come talk to me." He leaned over and kissed me on my forehead.

"I don't have nothing to say, Onyx. I need to go home."

"Why are you in a rush to go back to that nigga who put his fuckin' hands on you?"

My mouth fell open wide. "You don't know what you are talking about."

"I know a lot. More then, you know." He said as he pulled out my phone, waving it in front of me. "Now, eat your food." He left out of the room without saying another word, leaving me stuck with my mouth wide open.

At this point, I don't know what to do. On one hand, I can do as I was told and not have to worry about being abused. Then, on the other hand, I leave and deal with consequences, I know that awaiting me back home.

I grabbed the bag of food and made myself comfortable. I've been looking for a way to leave Aiden, and this might just be it. However, the last thing I want Onyx to think that him and I will be in a relationship. I've been tied to Aiden for so many years, and at this point, I just want to be single. I'm broken, and the only way I know I can repair myself is being by myself. I just hope Onyx can understand that.

Situations

Onyx

Sitting outside of Michelle's house, I found myself trying to find just what to say to her. It's been two days since I left her house. Two days since Trinity has been at my house and even though, I don't know how much longer she is going to stay. I know I need to fix things with Michelle before I even pursue anything with Trinity. Getting back with Trinity is something I know won't happen overnight. However, I want to be able to give her my all and not have to worry about any 'baggage.'

I know Trinity has been through so real fucked up shit that she has yet to tell me about. Even after I drilled her damn near all last night, she still refused to tell me what the fuck really happened. I let the shit go, for now. But whether she likes it or not, she will tell me what the fuck happened to her.

The vibration of Trinity's phone got my attention. I chuckled to myself as I watched the fuck nigga continue to call her phone back to back. I knew it was her dude because she had him save under 'MyHeart.' Nigga has been calling so much; I damn near answered the phone last night to tell him stop calling but, I thought against it. I will get my time with this bitch ass nigga soon. I through her phone in the glove compartment and got out of my car.

As I walked towards the front door, I thought about what I would say that wouldn't fuck up the friendship that we have. At the end of the day, I still would like to be friends with her. She was the only person I had in my corner for the last remaining years I had on sentence. She was there for me when I need someone the most.

I used my key; she gave me to enter the house. The faint smell of bacon hit me as I made my way into the house. I covered my nose because the smell of pork makes my stomach turn.

"Michelle, where you at?" I called out. I got no response and just followed the funky smell of the bacon. As I walked to the kitchen, I noticed the dishes were piled up in the sink, and the kitchen was a mess. Food containers were left all on the counters. Knowing how much of a clean freak Michelle is, I knew something couldn't be right.

I turned to leave out the kitchen to go and find Michelle and walked right into her.

"Damn, my bad I didn't-"

"What are you doing here?" She asked, cutting me off.

I gave her a once over and saw that she looked a mess. Her natural hair was matted to her head, the nightgown she wore was two sizes too big with food stains all over it, and she had dark circles around her eyes.

Seeing her in this condition made me instantly feel like shit. I know it's because of my disappearing act and that alone fucked with my head. Hurting Michelle is something I never wanted to do. However, I have to be honest with myself and her.

"Michelle, I need to talk to you."

She shook her head. "I already know. You don't want to be with me." She said as she brushed past me and headed over to the refrigerator. I watched as she pulled out a bottle of wine, opened it, and began to drink it straight from the bottle.

"Can we sit down so I can explain it to you, please? I owe you this."

She pulled the bottle from her lips and burst into a fit of giggles. "No nigga, what you owe me is the time I wasted on yo' bitch ass!" Her words slurred, and I knew she was already drunk.

I tried to reach for the bottle, but she quickly snatched it out of my grasp. "Come on, Michelle. This isn't even like you, ma'. Let me clean you up." I told her as I pulled her into my body.

WHAM!

Michelle slapped me so hard my ears were ringing. It took every-thing in my body not to hit her ass back.

"Let me go!" Michelle yelled as she tried to get out of my grasp, but the grip I had on her was too tight.

I was slowly losing my patience with Michelle. I know I'm the reasons behind her drinking and shit but, she is a grown fuckin' woman. She needs to carry herself as such.

"Chill the fuck out before I do some shit I might regret."

"What more can you do to me, huh? You've already broken me. I love you! I'm the one who held you down for four years! Where was she at when you needed something, huh? Answer me!" She yelled with tears falling from her eyes. I didn't respond. There was nothing that I could tell her that wouldn't make her feel better. I damn sure not about to talk to her in this state.

I need to be able to have this well needed conversation with her when she is in her right mind frame.

I let out a deep sigh and just swooped her up in my arms. I carried her to her bedroom. "Leave me alone, Damon. Go back to that whore you left me for."

"Shhhh. Chill out, Michelle." I whispered in her ear.

The more she cried, the more I felt like shit for doing her like this. She didn't deserve this, and I should have been a man about this shit years ago. Seeing her in this much pain made me wish I could go back in time and change this. However, that isn't an op-tion. The only thing I can do right now is right, my wrongs.

Michelle

My entire body was numb as I sat on my bed, just staring at the wall. Damon coming back here was like a slap in my face. He left my house two days ago without a word. Now, he's here trying to offer me up some lame-ass excuse when he knows deep down; I deserve more than that.

The last two days, I haven't been able to do nothing. I called out from work because there was no way I could function and deal with the type of bullshit that my jobs bring with all this on my mind.

The only thing I could think about is where did I go wrong? I thought I was the perfect or almost perfect woman for him. I guess not. I really had to take a moment and be honest with myself. The truth is, most men don't play around when it comes to what they want. When a man meets the woman who he spends the rest of his life with, he will waste no time making that woman his forever.

That's when I realized Onyx never said he wanted to marry me. He never talked about building a family together. I was just too blind to see it then. I was blinded by love, that I thought was real.

Falling in love is meant to be a two-sided love story. I love him, and he knows it but, it doesn't matter because he loves her. No matter what I try to do to get him to fall for me, it will never work because it will always be Her.

I should have been down with his ass when he dissed me at the restaurant. I should have never answered the phone when he called. I should have never helped him with his daughter. I shouldn't have done all the shit I did for him.

Onyx swooped me into his arms and carried me off towards my

bathroom. "Let me take care of you." He whispered in my ear.

I wanted to protest and scream until he put me down, but, at this point, I no longer had any fight left inside me. The sadness I felt isn't the kind where you cry all the time. No, it's the type of sadness that overwhelms my entire body. My heartache and my stomach are empty. I'm tired yet; I can't sleep.

All this behind a man who swore he would never hurt me. Now that I think about it, I remember I told him how my last relationship ended. He promised me that he would never do that to me. I mean, he didn't do exactly what Drew did, but, in the same sense, he is leaving me for another woman.

Onyx sat me down on the counter and slowly began to strip me out of my clothes. "What are you doing?" I snapped at him. There was a point where I craved to be around him now, just the sight of him makes me sick to my stomach.

"Relax. Let me get you cleaned up. I promise you will feel better after a hot bath."

I scoffed, "Like you actually care how I feel or not. Just leave and go back to her."

He let out a loud sigh. "I'm really trying to keep my cool and be understanding. But, you about to piss me off!"

Something inside my head snapped, and I hop down from the counter and just began to swing wildly, hitting him anywhere I could. "I hate you! I hate you!" I screamed over and over as I continued hitting him. I wanted him hurt, the same as I did.

"Chill the hell out, Michelle."

I should have taken heed to the tone of his voice, but the blind rage consumed me. "Nigga, I don't give a fuck-" My words were cut off when Onyx's large hands wrapped around my neck, and he slammed me hard against the door.

"Calm yo' ass down, listen, and shut the fuck up! I'm sorry, Michelle. If I can go back in time and change everything I would yet, things don't work like that. If you feel used or abandoned, I'm sorry. I truly am. I do love you but, not in the way you think. I love as a best friend. You were the only person by my side outside of Tanz when I was behind those walls. I do love you, Michelle. I just don't love you the way you deserve. You have to understand I am not the man for you."

All I could do was break down and cry. Hearing him saying that broke me to my core. What really hurt the most is that I knew he was telling the truth. One thing about Onyx, he always speaks the truth. Not once have this man lied to me. I might have taken what he's said switched it around to benefit me. But he has never lied to me.

I wiped the tears that had fallen from my eyes and pulled myself together. I have to stop feeling sorry for myself because, at the end of the day, I have to realize that my tears mean nothing. I'm still going to be alone and broken.

The saddest thing about love is that it cannot last forever, but the heartbreak always stays with you. As much as I don't want to say goodbye to Onyx, I know that it's a must. I know one day I will find a man to call my own; until then, I will focus on healing my heart.

$$\mathcal{Feelings.\,.\,.}$$

Aiden

"The only thing we've found was her car in the parking lot of the Walgreens."

"And the video footage?"

"Nothing. The only cameras they have is facing the front of the store, and her car was found on the side of the building. I can try pulling some of the other video footage from around the area."

"Yeah, do that." I ended the call before he could say anything else to piss me off.

It's been five days since Trinity's so-called disappearance. I thought after the way I beat her ass, she would have learned her lesson by trying to play with me. Then again, I guess I was wrong.

The more that I think about the things I've done to Trinity, I start to understand why she is acting out. Our relationship isn't what it used to be. I'm not the same man I was when I first met Trinity and Trinity isn't the same woman I met. In the beginning, we were just two young people looking for love. Now that we have both matured, we have two different visions on what we want in a partner. Her juvenile behavior is something I don't want in a wife. I can't be in a marriage with a woman who can't communicate with me.

As much as I don't want to, I'm going to have to the towel in. This relationship is starting to be more stressful, damn near toxic, then it should be. I have become a man that I don't even recognize. I wasn't raised to be the type of man to lay hands on his woman. If my mama knew that I was doing, she would kill me.

My phone ringing grabbed my attention. I looked at the screen and saw Kianna's name flash across.

I swiped left to answer, "What?" I answered.

"Well damn what crawled in yo' ass."

"What the fuck do you want? I'm not in the mood!"

"Calm down I'm just calling to see what is wrong with Trinity. I've been calling her for almost a week now." Exhaling loudly, I ended the call without answering her.

Before I could sit my phone down, she was calling me again. Reluctantly, I answered. "Trinity left me! I don't where she is!" I yelled into the phone. The line was quiet. I had to look at the phone to see if she had hung up. "Hello?"

"Um yeah, I'm here." She sounded confused, which lead me to believe she knows something about where Trinity could be.

"Um, what? Do you know where she is? Because if so, you have the right to tell me!" I shouted.

"Listen, Aiden; I don't owe you shit. My loyalty is to Trinity, not you."

"Well, how loyal are you to Trinity, when she doesn't know that you're married to her fiancé? Huh? Or the fact that you haven't signed the divorce papers that I've sent? How many copies do you have now?" As soon as those words left my mouth, Kianna ended the call.

Kianna needs to be truthful to herself. Yes, Trinity and her have been friends before I even came into the picture. However, the minute Trinity introduced us; she should have come clean then instead of begging me to keep it a secret.

At this point, I'm over both Trinity and Kianna. If Trinity

doesn't want to be with me, then so be it. It's time that I move on with my life.

Kianna

I downed a glass of Hennessy then quickly poured me another one. My hands were shaking so bad I was spilling the liquor everywhere. Hearing him bring up that we are married made me remember all the heartbreak I endured with him.

I met Aiden my freshman year at LSU. I was in a new state with no family or friends. My roommate was never around, so I was basically alone. One day I went to the library to study and bumped into Aiden literally. I wasn't paying attention to where I was walking; I was too busy texting that I ran right into him.

His dark brown eyes behind those Calvin Klein glasses pulled me right in. The expensive cologne he wore danced around my nostrils told me he was way out of my league and if I messed with him. I studied him, the way he moved, talked, and acted. I knew he came from money. He was definitely out of my league. The only thing he probably wanted from me was what I held in between my thighs.

I was used to that anyway. I never had a guy show me the type of attention that Aiden did. Guys back home only wanted me for one thing. But it wasn't all their fault. I made a name for myself in high school. I was too busy trying to fill a void in my life that I didn't realize I was being used by all the boys. The boys who claimed to 'want to be with me.' By the time I realized I was being used, it was too late. I already made a name for myself, which is one of the reasons I choose to go to a school out of state. I need a fresh start where no one knew me.

Instead of listening to my gut, I was stuck to him like glue. Every time you saw me, you saw Aiden. Our 'friendship' quickly turned into a relationship. Over the months, Aiden and I became close. Spring break came around, and Aiden took me to Las Vegas. What was supposed to be a week of fun quickly turned into my honeymoon?

One drunken night, Aiden and I was walking down Vegas strip. I made a joke about getting married, and three hours later, I became Mrs. Aiden Coleman. I remember being so happy in Vegas, I was on a cloud, and I was never coming down from. For the first time in my life, I had someone to love me for me. Even with my past, he still loved me. True Aiden and I had only been dating for a few months; I knew I made the right decision about marrying him. Everything about him was right, and adding the fact that he had money was only a bonus. I was ready to go back to school to focus on my studies and be the best wife I can be. Well, that was until we made it back to campus.

I fell from that cloud fast and hard. Aiden became a man I didn't recognize. He was a liar, cheater, and abusive. He thought that he could do whatever he wanted to do because, in the end, he would buy me an expensive gift, everything will be okay. Aiden took me through it to the point where I almost took my life.

Now fast forward years later, I'm still married to him. Yes, he's sent the divorce papers numerous times over the years, and after all the pain I experienced with him, one would think I would sign them papers quick, right?

Wrong.

Every time it's time for me to sign them papers, I freeze up. I don't know what's holding me back. I fell out of love with Aiden years ago, so why couldn't I sign those papers? Maybe it was because, to this day, he funded my lifestyle. True to his vows, Aiden made sure I wanted for nothing. He paid my rent, car note, and utilities. Maybe that's one of the reasons I didn't sign the papers.

I down my glass of Hennessey and pour me another one. My thoughts drifted to Trinity. I should have told her when she first introduced me to Aiden that he and I was married. But I bring myself to do it. She had been through a rough time after her first love broke her heart. For years she gave up on love, and when Aiden came into her life, something about my friend changed. For the first time in forever, she was happy. Who was I to take that from her? So, I decided against and kept the secret.

However, as the years past, I watched my friend slowly become a replica of me when I was with Aiden. I knew the signs that she displayed of happiness, confusion, and battered.

So naturally, I tried everything in power to get her to leave yet, she stayed. Each time, the same as I did. Part of me wanted her to leave him because I knew he meant her no good, and the other half couldn't woman up and tell her the real reason why I didn't want them together.

How was I supposed to tell my friend that I was already married to her fiancé, and I will be the reason she will never fully be Mrs. Aiden Coleman? I pondered over the thought of telling her the truth many of times. Yet, I could never go through with it.

Now, all of that doesn't even matter anymore. I'm glad she left Aiden, and I hope wherever she is with someone who deserves her. I am just glad that I will never have to tell her the truth about Aiden and me. My secret will forever be safe.

Finding me. . .

One Month Later. . .

Trinity

No one wishes to have dark days, sleepless nights, grumpy mornings, and this endless dark tunnel with no sign that it will end. I laid in this unfamiliar bed day in and day out. My semi-perfect life has shattered right before my eyes. The man who I thought I was going to spend the rest did the most disrespectful shit any man could do to a woman.

What makes matters worse, I fear the possibility that there might be something that could tie me to Aiden forever. However, I am not ready to learn the truth.

The door to the room I stayed in opened, and the faint smell of breakfast invade my nostrils.

"Trinity, come on, Ma' you need to eat something." Onyx voiced boomed throughout the room.

I clenched onto the covers tightly because, as good as the food smells, I still couldn't bring myself to eat it. Just the smell of it caused my stomach to turn, which only made my worse fears come true.

The covers being snatched off me got my attention quick. Standing at the end of the bed was Onyx wearing a frown. "Get up." He demanded.

I gave him a blank stare. The last time I talked to him was the day he brought me here. That same day I felt like I lost a piece of me. Getting away from Aiden should have been a blessing after how he treated me yet, here I am broken.

Not responding to him, I reached to grab the covers, so I can go back to hiding. Onyx quickly snatched the covers and threw them onto the floor.

"I said, get up." He demanded again.

I didn't respond. I laid back down in the bed and stared at the wall. "No," I mumbled.

"I wasn't giving you an option. Get. Up." He ordered. The tone of his voice caused something to snap in my head. The trauma I experience with Aiden caused me to feel anger and rage.

I jumped up from the bed and marched over to where he stood at the end of the bed. "I said, no! Now, leave me alone!" I yelled. I've had about all I can take of men telling me what I can and can't do. Treating like I was, I'm not a person. I've had just about enough of their bullshit.

Onyx stood there with a wide smirk on his face. I hated that he was so damn handsome. He stood in from of me, looking like a tall glass of chocolate milk, and I was dying for a sip. Quickly shaking those thoughts from my head, I put my focus back to why I was smiling.

"What's so damn funny?" I had to know.

"You." He replied.

"Me?" I was confused.

"You listened to me." I stood there, confused. He was talking in circles instead of just coming out and saying what he meant. I guess he sensed that I didn't understand. "I see you got yo' ass out the bed." I stood there, feeling dumb.

I turned to make my way back to the bed when he grabbed my wrist, stopping me. "Trinity, we need to talk."

I quickly snatched away from him. I didn't like the way his

touch felt. It was warm and welcoming. Familiar. Yet, the last thing I need right now is to be caught up with Onyx again.

"There is nothing to talk about. Now, if you don't mind, I would like to go back to sleep."

Nah, ain't no more sleeping. You've been stuck in this room for a month. It's time for you to get yourself together."

I scoffed. "Until you know what I've been through, then you can judge me."

"Ain't nobody judging you. If you would just tell me what happened, maybe I could help you." I cut my eyes at him. Help me? Can't nobody help me? I allowed myself to get into this situation, and I am the only person that can get myself out of this.

"Oh, I've overstayed my welcome. Well, you can take me to my parent's house. I'm sure they are worried sick about me anyway."

He shook his head. "That's not what I was saying. Look eat your food, take a shower, and then we can talk about it."

I narrowed my eyes at him. The authority he spoke made me feel things I haven't felt in a long time. Feelings that only he can make me feel. I didn't like that he still held some kind of hold onto me. I am not the same naïve girl he once knew. I'm a grown woman that knows what she does and doesn't want. Also, I know how I want to be treated. Onyx can't just tell me what to do and think that he is going to have some sort of control over me. From this day forward I will do what Trinity wants to do.

I folded my arms across my chest and shook my head. "No. I told you I don't want to eat."

Onyx moved to where I was standing by the bed. He towered my small frame making me regret even opening my mouth. I instantly drop my head down afraid to even look him in his eye. I forgot just how intimating the presence can be.

He lowered towards my ear and whispered, "Either you eat the food or I' ma make you eat. I have allowed you to act this wat for far too long. You know exactly what I am capable of, so I suggest you get yo' act together before I make you." The warmth of his breathe sent chills down my spine. His words were harsh and cold. Never have I experienced him speak to me this way. I wanted to apologize for my actions but, by the time I looked up all I saw was the back of him as he left out of the room.

I slumped down onto the bed confused. The way Onyx made me feel left me confused. I looked over at the breakfast he had prepared for me and gagged.

I quickly rushed to the bathroom and threw up last night's dinner all over the floor. I cursed myself because this is the third time I've done this. It's bad enough that I'm throwing up, but even worse when I have to clean.

The room became hot, and my vision became blurry. I knew I haven't been taking care of myself lately, but this was more than just a cold or sickness. The fear of what Aiden had done to me was coming back to hunt me.

My thoughts went back to the day I ran into Onyx. Three days, Aiden raped me repeatedly, filling me with his seeds. As he beat me, he told me that if I didn't get pregnant soon, that he would find someone else to carry his child and make me take care of it, as if I was its mother. I prayed every time he came in me that I wouldn't get pregnant. The last thing I need was to birth his child. That alone would tie me together with him forever. I know Aiden never let me go if I am pregnant.

I went to the Walgreens, seeking out the plan b pill. There was no way in hell that I would want to carry his child. Just the thought of that alone caused my stomach to turn. I rushed to the toilet and continued to throw up my guts.

"Trinity-" Onyx voice behind me caused my body to freeze.

I slowly turned around to see him standing there with a blank expression. He looked at the throw up then back at me. I cursed myself for not locking the door when he left.

"Onyx I-I can explain..." Burp. My head found its way back into the toilet.

I felt his presence behind me. My body shook as I emptied the rest of the continence in my stomach.

His big warm hand rubbed my back as I laid across the toilet.

"I'm sorry for upsetting you." He whispered. "I'm sorry for yelling at you. I didn't mean to make you sick. I promise to never leave your side."

The tears that pooled my eyes finally fell freely. The fact that Onyx felt he was the reason I was throwing was because of him. Little does he know this has nothing to do with him. However, after I find out the truth out about my situation, I'm sure he won't be by my side like he claims he will.

<p align="center">~~~</p>

Standing in front of the mirror, I cringed at the reflection staring back at me. I was no longer the once outgoing and vibrant Trinity I used to be. The woman I saw in the mirror was broken and tired. I still can't believe I allow a man to turn me into this person I hardly even recognized. I don't know how I allowed a man to gain so much control over me that made me turn into this woman who I didn't know.

Taking a deep breath, I exhaled all of the trauma I've endured these last few months. It's time that I take control back of my life, which will start with finding out if I am pregnant or not. Officially.

I slid on the clothes that Onyx bought for me. He was so thoughtful. The panty and bra set he bought be showed that he cared. They might have been the wrong size but, it's okay. The Adidas sweatsuits he got for me was a little too big, but that alright. It's the thought that counts. Just the thought of Onyx made me thankful for him allowing me into his home. He cooked for me and cared for me when I wasn't able too. He didn't pressure me anymore since the incident in the bathroom. I still haven't been able to talk to him. I don't think I will ever be able to talk. I will forever be thankful to him, but it's time for me to leave. I've overstayed my welcome, and I can't just be a burden in his life anymore.

He has a young daughter who he has to care for and doesn't need me being in the way with that. I'll just have him take me to my parents' house, and I'll figure out my life from there.

As I finished getting dressed, I looked at the wild natural mane, on the top of my head, I called hair. I did the best messy bun I could do without any hair care product. The first thing I am going to do is make me a hair appointment. It was well overdue.

I gathered the little bit of my stuff that I had here and stuffed it into a plastic bag. I gathered my stuff and walked out of the room that I've locked myself in for the last month.

Walking down the stairs, I heard Onyx's deep voice coming from the kitchen. I made my way towards the kitchen but stopped when I realized that he wasn't alone. He was in the middle of a conversation with a man I had never seen before. I quickly took in the guy's appearance, the baggy pants and oversized shirt made me remember just what that Onyx did for a living. The reason he was taken away from me.

Onyx clearing his throat pulled from my thoughts. I didn't even realize him, and his company were staring at me.

"You alright, Ma' you need something?" The way Onyx was staring at me, reminded me of when we first met. He always looked at me as if he could see my soul. I used to always find myself lost in those big, dark brown eyes of his.

I pulled my eyes from his and looked over at his company. "Um… I see you busy; it's okay. I'll wait."

"Oh, this my brother from another mother, Tanz. Tanz, this my

Trinity, my Ol' lady."

I shook Tanz hand then realized what Onyx just said. "Excuse me? Ol' lady?" I placed my hands on my hips and mugged him. He walked up on me smiling, showing off that one sexy dimple. "Tanz, I'll get up with you later." He said to him, never taking his eyes off mine.

His stare was intense and making me feel things I know I shouldn't. The cologne he was wearing I cleared my throat and took a step back but, he wrapped his strong arm around me, pulling me back closer to him.

"Where are you going dressed up looking all good?"

I tried to remove his arm from around me, but he wasn't letting go. "Can you let me go?" I hissed.

"Answer my question first." I knew the only way to get him to let me go was to answer him.

"I wanted to see if you can bring me to my parents' house."

"To visit?" He asked then his eyes fell to my bag I was holding. His eyes met mine again and I saw a flash of hurt in them. "Damn, just like that, huh? You just go walk out the door and leave?" He even sounded hurt.

"I have stayed here long enough; it's time that I got back to my life."

"Your life? The life where you were some bitch ass nigga's punching bag?" I removed his arm from around me, and this time, he didn't put up a fight.

"Wow. Um… I'll just see myself out." I turned and walked away. As I reached for the door handle, I stopped and looked back at where Onyx was. He had yet to move from where he stood. A chuckle slipped from my throat. For some reason I thought that he would have been right there behind me, begging me to stay. However, that wasn't the case.

I shook my head and let myself out of his house. The Dallas cold hit me directly in my face taking my breath away with it.

I closed my eyes, inhaled deeply, and exhaled everything I've been holding onto this last month. When I opened my eyes, I felt like I could finally see the world for the first time. Yet, I was still uncertain about what my future holds. I can't follow my heart because it's just as confusing as my mind. However, two things I know for sure is that I won't go back to Aiden, and I will get back to being

Risk It All. . .

Onyx

I waited for her to bring her ass back into the house. I looked down at the time on my phone, and she had been gone for about ten minutes now. It's sixty degrees outside, so; I know her ass is cold. That sweat suit ain't go be able to keep her ass warm.

I know I shouldn't have said what I said, but, shit it was the truth. That nigga beat her ass like she was a nigga on the street, blacking her both of her eyes trying to kill her beauty; instead, he killed her spirit. Shawty laid her ass in that damn bed for an entire month. She barely ate or showered. That nigga broke her, and if that's who she wanted to be with, who am I the one to stop her?

I put up with her nasty ass attitude and dealt with the cold shoulder for an entire month. I washed her ass without her, even asking me. I did the shit because there was no way that I can just leave her like that. Even with all that, I still made sure she had everything she needed while she was here, and that's how she wants to act? Then so be it. I have never chased behind a female in my life, and I'm not about to start today.

I turned around to head to my bedroom. I made it to the first step and quickly turned around and rushed out of the house. "Fuck!" I hissed as I rushed down to the sidewalk and looked left and right. I didn't see Trinity.

I might talk my shit but, I can't let her crazy ass just walk in this cold. I quickly jumped into my truck to go find her. I know she has been through some traumatic stuff, and I know I should handle her with care but, when she said she was ready to get back to her life, I felt some type of way.

I thought once she got her mind right that maybe she and I could start back where we left off, only this time as adults. I want the chance to learn how to love this new Trinity.

I hit the corner and saw Trinity walking towards the bus stop. I still can't believe that this crazy-ass girl really took off walking, not even knowing what part of town she was in. I do stay on the good side of Dallas still; nowadays, you never know what could happen.

I parked my car and got out. I need to make shit right with Trinity. Deep down, I know that Trinity was made for me; she just doesn't know it yet.

As I walked towards the bus stop, I heard Trinity soft cries. It pained me to know that she was hurt because of some shit I said to her. She's been through enough with that fuck nigga; she doesn't need me adding to the bullshit.

"Trinity, come on, and let's go."

Her head snapped up. "What? No, leave me alone."

"Look, I'm sorry-"

"I don't care." She said, cutting me off. I had half of the mind to snatch her ass up and drag her to the car. Then again, that would only make shit worse.

I sat down next to her and grabbed her hand. "Look, I'm sorry. Let me take you where you need to go. It's too cold for you to be sitting out here."

"I'm good, Damon, you can go." Her calling me by my government name caught me off guard. She has never called me by my government name.

"Damon, huh?"

"Yep. Now leave me alone."

Chuckling, I rubbed her hand, trying my best to stay calm, but her little attitude is starting to get on my nerves. This back and forth, shit are getting old to me. I am a man who likes the chase. However, Trinity ass is stubborn as a bull. She doesn't understand my way of thinking, and that's okay. I rather show her and not tell her.

I pull Trinity into my arms, picked her up, and carried her towards my car.

"Onyx put me down!" She screamed. Her screams and punches didn't faze me. I'm not about to go back and forth with her ass anymore.

I pushed her ass into the backseat of my truck and quickly shut the door.

"Let me out!" She yelled, banging on the window.

A chuckle slipped my throat when I realized that she couldn't get out because the door was on child lock.

I jumped into the truck and was met with a hard punch to the head.

Wham!

"Don't you ever grab me like that again!"

Stunned wouldn't describe how I felt. I can't believe Shawty caught me off guard like that.

Rubbing my face, I smiled. "You hit like a girl."

She scoffed and rolled her eyes. "Want me to do it again?" She snapped.

"Next time you lay your hands on me is when I have you in my bedroom," I told her before I started the car and pulled off towards my house.

The entire ride back to my house was quiet. She hadn't

said anything else about taking her to her parents' house, and I wasn't about to suggest it. As I pulled in front of my house, I watched Trinity in the rearview mirror; she still had that empty look in her eyes.

I didn't know how to approach her to even see what I can do to make things better. I've asked myself over and over why I am putting all this work into her when there is no guarantee that she is going to love me the way she used too. Then I realize that the is a reason she was bought back into my life. Only this time, I won't allow anything to tear us apart.

I placed my car in park and killed the engine. "Are you going to come inside?"

She shrugged.

I let out a deep sigh before I got out of the car. I'd had about all I can take of Trinity's shit. I was about to open her car door, then I thought about how nasty she has been towards me when I haven't done anything to her. I do want to be with her, but, at the same time, she got me fucked up if she thinks, I'm about to just kiss her ass.

I turned and walked towards the house. She is going to learn real soon that I always get what I want. No matter the cost. I'll risk everything I have for her, even if that means showing her that I'm with all the shits too.

Afraid of change . . .

Trinity

I sat in confusion and watched as Onyx walked into the house and shut the door, leaving me in this car.

"I know he didn't leave me in this car," I said out loud to myself. I went to open the car door then I realized he must have had the child lock on. This shit he was doing is childish.

I still can't believe that I am back here, but at the same time, a part of me wanted to be here. Even with all the shit I went through with Aiden; I should hate men. However, Onyx showed me that there are a few decent men still out there. At the same time, I don't know if I'll ever be able to be in another relationship again. How am I supposed to trust another man again?

I climbed into the front seat and let got out of the truck. Thoughts of being with Onyx again came into play. Just as those thoughts came to me, I pushed them to the back of my mind. I need to focus on figuring out my own current situation first before I ever entertain the thought. At the same time, I don't know if I will ever be able to trust another man with my heart.

If Onyx wants to be with me, he will have to understand me and take things slow. He can't expect me to just jump into another relationship when I'm just getting out one. Aiden put me through some shit no woman should ever endure with a man who claims to love her. I know I can't allow what Aiden did to me

I entered the house and ran right into Onyx hard chest. My eyes met his, and I saw a hint of sadness in them. However, his face held no expression. "Onyx, we need to talk."

"We do?" He asked sarcastically.

"Um… yes. I owe it to you. Can we sit down?"

He grabbed my hand and led me over to the couch. My stomach was turning flips, thinking about the conversation I was about to have with him. I promised myself that I would never tell anyone about what Aiden did to me. The shit was degrading and embarrassing. However, I know in order for Onyx to understand me fully, I have to tell him what I've been through.

"I-I…" Clearing my throat, I started again. "I don't even know where to start. I am, well, I mean, I was engaged to be married but, things just weren't right. Aiden was the first guy I dated after you left me. In the beginning, everything was perfect. He helped me love again. Then after he asked me to marry him, things slowly start to change. He became controlling, possessive, unsatisfiable, and abusive. I took it all because I feared that I would never find another man to love me. Well, honestly, I just didn't want to go through the entire relationship thing with someone else, so I stayed. Until the day I tried on my dress for its final fitting. Something inside told me not to marry him. I'd been having the feeling for months yet; it wasn't until I put that damn dress on. I knew that I couldn't marry him, and if I did marry him, I would live a life of unhappiness." Tears fell from my eyes, and I didn't bother wiping them. This was my truth, and in order for me to move forward, I need to tell my story. "The day I went home from my final dress fitting, I was going to tell Aiden I didn't want to be with him any longer. I loved him, but I wasn't in love with him anymore. That's the same night when he began to beat me and…" My words trailed off as I thought about what I was about to say next. I don't know how he's going to react.

"And what?" His deep voice caused me to jump.

"Um… He raped me. For three whole days." My silent cries

turned into loud sobs. "The things he did to me. . . I-I... I didn't deserve that." I finally broke down and cried. "No woman should ever have to deal with that, especially from a man who claimed to love her."

I cried for the abuse I endure. I cried for the love that was lost. I cried for the life that I once had was over. These weren't tears of sadness; these were tears of freedom. Telling my truth made me finally feel free for the first time in a very, very long time.

Onyx wrapped his arms around me and held me tightly. His embrace was warm, familiar, and for the first time in a long time, I felt safe.

"Shhh. Stop all that crying. You won't ever have to worry about that nigga again. That's my word."

"T-there is something else I need to tell you."

His body stiffed. "What?

I wiped my face then turned to face him. I need to see his reaction when I tell him this. I don't know how this will make things between us different. "I think I might be pregnant," I confessed.

I watched his widen; then his eyes fell down to my stomach.

"The day I went to Walgreens, I was there to get a plan b pill. I can't have his baby, Onyx I just can't."

He didn't respond.

We both sat in silence, lost in our own thoughts. I was worried about what he was thinking. After sitting for about ten minutes, I stood from the couch. It's obvious that Onyx isn't feeling the fact that I might be pregnant, and I understand that. I can't expect him to accept me at my lowest point and pregnant at that.

I started to walk away when Onyx grabbed my wrist. "Sorry about my reaction. I just wasn't expecting you to say that. I can't believe that nigga would do some shit like that. Look, I'm about to go to the store and get a couple of pregnancy tests, and we will go from there, okay?"

"We?" I asked, and he nodded.

He grabbed my hands and pulled me into his hard body. "Look, I know that you've been through some fucked up shit with that fuck nigga but, I'ma let you know this right now. I am not him." He stared into my eyes with those big, dark brown eyes. His words hit me harder than they should have. He didn't say much but, what he did say struck a nerve inside of me.

"Onyx, I don't want you-"

He cut me off by placing his finger on my lips. "Shhh... Relax and go upstairs. I'll be back in a few. Stop stressing; it's not good for you, my baby." He walked away, leaving me standing in the same spot stuck. I can't believe what he said.

When I first came inside this house, I planned on telling him my truth; that's it. I didn't expect for him to claim a child that he knows that is not his. I don't even know where to go from here.

~ ~ ~

I sat on the toilet, holding the pregnancy test box in my hand. I looked up, and Onyx was standing the by the bathroom door staring at me with those dark brown eyes. "Are you just going to stare at me the entire time? I mean, can I have some privacy?" I mumbled nervously.

"Nope." He quickly replied. "In this relationship, we don't have any privacy."

I cocked my head to the side and gave him a funny look. "What-"

He raised his hand, stopping me. "Take the damn test, Trinity."

I waited for him to leave yet; he never did. Sighing loudly, I decided to finally get this over with. Taking the test out of the box, my heart was beating hard out of my chest.

I removed the cap off the test, took a deep breath, and peed in the stick. I sat the test on the counter, finished wiping myself, and flushed the toilet. I made my way to the sink to wash my hands, and Onyx was right by my side.

"How long do we have to wait."

I shrugged. "Three minutes, maybe less." He nodded.

Silence fell between us, and I know that we were both lost in our own thoughts. The seconds that passed felt like hours. "I-I can't look at it," I told him. He nodded and grabbed the test.

I watched him like a hawk when he read the results. A smile slowly crept across his face, and I didn't know how to take that. He flipped the test facing me, and the words pregnant was staring back at me.

It felt as if I've been hit by a bus looking at the results. The tears I've been holding back finally broke free, and I burst into a fit of sobs. Falling to the bathroom floor, I held my stomach and cried because there was no way in hell that I can have this baby.

I always wanted children; however, the thought of going back to being with Aiden made me sick to my stomach. My stomach rumbled, and before I knew it, I was throwing up all over the floor.

"Dammit Trinity, why are you crying? A child is a blessing." Onyx said while rubbing my back.

I pushed him away from me because I don't know how he is going to react by what I have to say. "I can't have this baby," I mumbled.

"Come again? I didn't hear you." Onyx moved closer to me.

"I can't have his child. If I have this baby, he will never leave me alone, and I'll be forced to marry him."

"Then, have my child."

"What?" I asked, confused.

"What if no one knows it's his child."

I shook my head. "Onyx, no. I can't allow you to take care of a child that isn't yours. It's not right."

"You not allowing me to do shit. I want to be the father; I am going to be the father."

"Why?" I questioned him. I had to know. I needed to know why he would do something for me, and we aren't even in a relationship.

He grabbed my hands and pulled me closer to him. "Trinity, I love you, and I have been in love with you since we first met. I know how much you want kids, and I can't let what that fuck nigga did you change that for you. I am willing to step up and be the father of our child, no matter what."

I broke down, crying even harder. Onyx wrapped his arms around me and held me tightly. Being in his arms, I found myself feeling comfortable. Being in his arms, I felt safe. Being in his arms, I finally felt at ease.

"Where do we go from here?"

"What do you mean?"

I pushed myself away from him. "I mean, what are we doing? I'm not trying to be ungrateful but, I-I feel deep down in my heart I am not ready for a relationship, and I'm not trying to lead you wrong."

He narrowed his eyes at me, and my stomach flipped. I just knew I said something wrong to piss him off. The last thing I need right now is for him to be upset with me.

"You can't lead me wrong when this is something I want to do. I know you ain't ready for me, and that's okay. I'm willing to wait as long as it takes because I know deep down inside you were made for me." Leaving me with nothing else to say, I laid my head against his chest, and for the first time in forever, I allowed myself just to let go.

Six Months Later. . .

Dreams are made to become a reality. . .

Trinity

Pulling up in front of my parents' house, I let out a deep sigh. I haven't seen them in months, and I don't know how they are going to feel about seeing me like this. Outside of my weekly phone calls and daily text, my parents have no clue that I'm seven and a half months pregnant. Being that I am their only child, they are going to freak out. Especially my mama.

I love my parents; however, these last six months, I took time to love and learn myself all over again. I literally had to disconnect myself from the world in order to get back to myself. I haven't even spoken to Kianna, which is weird, but I needed this time for myself.

Being with Onyx, he allowed me to quit my job and enrolled back into school full-time. I wanted to do both yet; he insisted that I focus on only school because he didn't want me to be stressed while pregnant.

Speaking of Onyx, this man was sent from God to me. Back when we were younger, the Onyx, I knew, was completely different from the man I wake up to every morning.

Onyx is gentle, loving, and attentive. He listened to me, learned what I didn't like, and took every word I saw into con-sideration. Everything that I begged Aiden for Onyx gave me with no questions and no title of a relationship. This man allowed me to be Trinity, nothing else. Every day I woke up, I was in complete bliss. Each day I was with Onyx, I felt better about the decision I made leaving Aiden.

For the last six months, my life with Onyx has become a routine. We would wake up; he would cook breakfast while Damiana and I got ready for the day. From the first day that I met Damiana, she was stuck to me like glue. At first, I thought she was going to feel some type of way about me being there yet; she did the complete opposite. After Onyx explained to me the situation with her mama, I understood why she clings to me. Honestly, I loved being around her just as much as she enjoyed being around me. She is such a smart, beautiful, smart little girl, and very well mannered.

Onyx placed his big hand on my swollen belly, snapping me out of my thoughts. "Relax, Pooh Bear; everything is going to be alright. You're going to stress my baby." Instantly the baby started to kick. As always, when he touches my stomach t was like he or she knew that it was him.

We decided to wait to know the baby's gender until birth; however, he was convinced that we were having a girl.

"I'm just nervous, that's all."

"You have no reason to now come on."

He jumped out of the car before I could say anything else. He walked over to my side of the car and helped me out of the car. Small things like this just made my heart jumped.

The minute I step out the car, my parent's front door flew open, and my mama rushed outside. "Trinity!" She screamed as she ran towards me.

"Shit," I mumbled to myself. I haven't even had the chance to think of how I'm going to explain to my parents about Onyx. Last, they knew I left Aiden; they had no idea about me living with Onyx.

My mama stopped a few feet away from me when she noticed my belly. Her hands flew up to her mouth. "Oh, My, Trinity, how? Am I going to be a GG?" She could barely get her words out as tears filled both of our eyes.

I nodded. "Yes." She pulled me into a hug, and the tears broke free. She pulled away from me, and her eyes slid over to Onyx then back to me.

"Is this who has been keeping you from your family?" She asked, eyeing Onyx up and down.

I opened my mouth to speak but, Onyx cut me off. "How are you doing, ma'am my name is Damon Warren, and I am Trinity's friend."

She looked at me with narrowed eyes. "Friend, huh?" She asked as she knew differently.

"Yes, ma'am." He replied with that million-dollar smile showing off that sexy dimple.

"Hmmm. Well, let's go into the house. We have a lot of catching up to do. Wait until your daddy sees you, he's going to have a heart attack." Hearing her say that made me nervous.

Onyx grabbed my hand and smiled. "Relax mama. Don't stress."

Smiling back at him, we both followed behind my mama into the house. I took a deep breath and mentally prepared for my overbearing parents.

~ ~ ~

"Mama that food was amazing, I really did miss your cooking." I grabbed the plates off the table and walked over to the sink. After my parents questioned and integrated both Onyx and me for two hours about our relationship status. We ate lunch before Onyx had to leave and go to work. I really thought that the conversation was going to south once I mentioned to them that Onyx was my child's father. My daddy was pissed! Onyx took him outside, and thirty minutes they walked back into the house as best friends.

I asked Onyx what they talked about, and he told me not to worry about it. I brushed it off and focused back on the conversation.

"Trinity, baby, sit down I got it." She said, trying to take the plates out of my hands.

"Ma' stop. I'm pregnant, not handicap. I got this."

"Speaking of that. When were you going to tell us you were pregnant, huh? After you had my grandchild?"

"No, ma'am. I-I just really needed to get back to me. After how things ended with Aiden, I just needed time to myself, you know?"

She nodded. "Hmmm. I bet that fine man in there had something to do with you getting back to yourself, huh?"

A smile slowly crept across my face. As much as I wanted to hide it, I couldn't. Onyx definitely does have a hand in helping me get back to myself. As much as Onyx is a God sent man, for some reason, I feel like things with him is just too good to be true. No matter how much I try to convince myself that, I'm just paranoid and not to think too much into it. It's always in the back of my mind that Onyx, one day will switch up on me the same way Aiden did to me.

"Mama, we are just friends, who just happened to have a baby on the way together."

"Whatever you say, Trinity. I know you hiding something from me but, you're grown, and I'm going to let you live your own life. But tomorrow I start shopping. Oh my, I don't even know what to buy? What would make you want to wait til' you give birth to find out the gender?" I shrugged.

For the next hour, we just talked about everything under the sun. I can tell my mama missed me just as much as I missed her. We were talking and laughing so much I didn't even realize that it was getting late.

I pulled out my phone and sent Onyx a text letting him know to pick me up.

I stood from the table to make my way to the bathroom when a knock on the front door grabbed my attention. I wobbled towards the front door, turned the locks, and without looking to see who it was, I opened the door and got the shock of my life when I saw who was on the other side.

I instantly became nervous and started to shake. Fear took over me, and the only thing I could think of was the last time he and I was together. The things he did to me played like a movie in my head.

Those light brown eyes that held the same shock expression as mine, quickly changed when they fell onto my stomach. His eyes met mine again. "Is it mine?" Was all that came out his mouth.

My biggest fear was for Aiden to see me pregnant; I knew the moment he saw me; he would put two and two together. Going back to Aiden is the last thing I want to do, especially since I am pregnant. If this man would put his hands on me, there is no telling what he would do to our child.

I opened my mouth to respond, but no words came out. "Answer me!" He yelled, causing me to jump in fear.

"No, it's mine." Onyx's deep voice got both of our attention.

My eyes met his, and I instantly felt safe. My baby began to kick like he or she knew that daddy was near. I placed a hand on my stomach and smiled. I know I said that I wasn't ready to be with Onyx in a relationship just yet. However, the way my body feels when he is close says another thing. My heart starts to race, and I instantly feel happy when I see his face says so much yet, I know I'm not ready mentally to be the woman he needs me to be.

Onyx pulled his eyes from me and turned his attention to Aiden.

They both locked eyes on each other. Seeing them both here together scared me. I know what both of them are capable of doing. Neither of them is the type to back down from a fight. Deep down, I know this will not end well.

In My Feelings. . .

Aiden

Her lips, her eyes, and the fact that she was standing in front of me big pregnant made my mind go a mile a minute. It's been six months since I've seen her and the day I decide to come to her parents' house to bring all her belongings she just so happens to be here.

After six whole months of living life as a bachelor, I thought that Trinity leaving was a sign that the end for us was a good thing. There is no day that have pass that I haven't thought about her. A piece of her was all over the house. Everywhere I turned, I saw something that reminded me of her. Which is the reason I am standing outside of her parents' house with my car full of her belongings. Yet, seeing her here makes the saying; when you love someone, let them go, and if it comes back, then you know true.

Since she left, I have been with a lot of women who are all faceless when it comes to comparing to Trinity. I have yet to find a woman who intrigued me enough to take my mind off Trinity. Maybe the time apart was what we needed to get back to us. Adding the fact that she's pregnant with my child also means something. However, the fact I have this unknown nigga standing behind me saying otherwise is fucking with my mental.

I turned and studied Trinity. She has to be around seven or eight months pregnant, which means that the baby this nigga is claiming is definitely mine. But the real question is, who is this dude to feel comfortable enough to claim a child he knows isn't his?

My eyes met hers again. "I'ma give you five, no two minutes to let this clown know who baby that is," I told her.

Her eyes widen. "Aiden. W-what are you doing here?"

"Trinity!" I turned to see the unknown man walk pass me to Trinity. He wrapped his arms around her round belly and whispered something in her. I watched the two of them together. A blind person could see there was chemistry between the two. I watch as her body relaxed with him, the sparkle in her eye that she once had was back yet, that sparkle was because of another man.

My blood began to boil as I thought about the last conversation I had with Trinity. She claimed to no be in love with me anymore or what not. How she wanted her own independence bullshit yet, here she is standing looking all in love with the next man.

Clearing my throat, both of them turned to face me. "Trinity let's go we have a lot of shit to discuss!"

"Y'all ain't got shit to discuss bro. So, go head and move around man, Trinity ain't yo' business no mo."

I step forward. "I said let's go-"

Click!

The sound of a gun cocking got our attention. We all turned our attention towards the front door, and there stood Trinity's daddy with a pistol in his hand, aimed in my direction.

"And I said she ain't going nowhere with you, son! So, go ahead in you about yo' business because I buss one in ya' ass!"

"Trinity you come with me or –"

Pow!

"That's a warning shot. Next one goes in ya' ass son!"

My eyes slid over to Trinity, and she smirked back at me like she won something. Her ass better have the same energy because this shit is far from over.

"This shit ain't over!" I pointed at her before I turned and ran back to my truck.

As I pulled from in front of the house, I dialed the only person that I know that I can count on when it comes to Trinity.

"What Aiden!" Kianna answered on the first ring. I'm sure she is in her feelings because ever since Trinity left, I stopped taking care of Kianna. I didn't have Trinity in my life, so there was no need to keep paying her to keep a secret that didn't matter anymore. Without my money as an extra income, Kianna was forced to do something she hasn't done in years; care for herself financially.

"Lighten up beautiful, look, I got a way you can make some money. Maybe enough money to go shopping just like you used to."

The line went quiet, which means her mind was turning. "What is it?"

A smile spread across my face because I knew she would take the bait. "I need you to make nice with Trinity again."

"That's it?"

"Yeah, and report back to me the way you used to."

Trinity can't hide behind her dad forever, especially when it comes to keeping me away from my child. She better hope, that child ain't mine because if it is, she is in for a rude awakening.

Am I The One For You. . .

Onyx

"You sure you alright, Trinity?" This had to be the third time I asked her since we left her parents' house.

"Yes, I told you I am." She replied. I could sense the attitude in her voice. Due to the circumstances, I' ma let the shit slid but, she knows I don't like her tone. I know with her pregnancy hormones, her mouth can become reckless.

I tried to focus on the road ahead of me, but thoughts of Trinity and her ex filled my head. I had left her parents' house for two hours, and all of a sudden, dude just shows up out the blue? Nah, I don't believe that there is a reason he was there, and I want to know.

"Why was he there?"

She shrugged. "I don't know." She answered nonchalantly.

"So, the nigga just showed up?" I was trying my hardest to keep my cool but, something in the back of my mind was telling me that it was more to the story than Trinity was telling me.

The last six months, Trinity and I have gotten closer. She began opening up to me more, expressing herself, and letting me know what she does and doesn't like. She quickly took on the role of a mother figure in Damiana's life without me, even asking.

I found myself falling for her more and more every day. Adding to the fact that I am able to experience her pregnancy with her. I don't know how much more I can just continue to be just friends. Now, with her ex popping up, I fear she might want to go back to him.

"Onyx, I don't know. He knocked on the door, I opened it, and you showed up that's it."

"WHY?" I banged my hand on the steering wheel. Jealousy was pumping through my body. I shouldn't feel this way because, at the end of the day, we aren't together. We haven't even had sex yet, because I know she might be physically ready for me, but she's not mentally ready. When it's time for us to become sexual, I want her to know that she is mine. Her body, mind, and soul belong to me. However, at the same time, I can't change the way I feel about her.

"What you're not about to do is yell at me. I told you the truth, and you can either accept it or not. I don't owe you no explanation. If you haven't forgotten, we are not together!"

"You know what, you're right." Was my only response.

Silence fell between us. There was nothing else to be said. My mind began to move a mile a minute, thinking about what could have caused Trinity to say that she just said. I've spent six months with this woman learning her likes and dislikes. Caring for her, learning her moods, and what makes her tick now, this nigga shows up she's back to the same Trinity that I met outside of the Walgreens. Nonchalant, secretive, and mean. I put too much work in breaking her out of that only for her to go right back to that.

I focused my attention back onto the road. Today was supposed to be a good day, and it turned to be fucked up. Tanz called, telling me there was an emergency at the shop, and when I got there, I walked right into Brooke on her best bullshit.

Eight months of Damiana leaving with me, I hadn't heard a peep from Brooke. Yet, the minute I have court paper petitioning for full custody. Now, she calls herself coming into my place of business starting drama. Knocking over Tv's and destroying property.

I was ready to go across her head then I realized that that's exactly what she wanted me to do. So, I played the game like she would. I called the Police, got the entire thing on a police report. I had to play the game smart just so I'll have a paper trail on her, which will make my court case easier. Brooke will never get Damiana back as long as I'm alive.

I looked over at Trinity, and I saw the stress lines forming on her forehead. I touched her thigh. "Relax mama. Stressing ain't good for my baby."

She pushed my hand off her. "Leave me alone." She spat.

"Yo' I've been trying to keep my cool with you but, you know I don't deal with that attitude shit!"

"Well, don't deal with it. Matter of fact take me back to my parents' house."

"Why? So, you can call that nigga to come back, and y'all make up and shit?"

"Maybe." She answered quickly.

Hearing her say that caused me to smash on the brakes bring the truck to an erupt stop in the middle of the street. Rage took over, and I felt myself slipping into a blind rage.

"What are you-"

"What the fuck did you just say to me?" I cut her off.

"Onyx we are in the middle of the street-"

"ANSWER ME!" I yelled.

I turned to face her and saw tears slowly build in her eyes. "Why are you yelling at me-"

"Trinity. Those tears mean nothing to me. Now, answer me. What. Did. You. Say?" I was trying my best to keep my cool but, with each passing second, I was losing all the patience I had left.

"I-I said." She paused as she wiped her tears. "I said maybe. B-But I-I didn't mean it, Onyx. I promise." She reached out to touch me, but I brushed her away.

She probably didn't mean it; however, she said what she said. "Bet." I unbuckled my seatbelt and jumped out of the car. "You want to be with that nigga, then go be with him." I heard her calling my name but, I didn't bother to go back. At this point, I could give two fucks about the truck or the fact that I'm seven miles away from my house or anything at this moment. Hearing her say that shit fucked with my mind and heart.

The way I feel right now is the same way I felt the night I went to jail. Heavy-hearted. The night she gave me her innocence, begged me not to break her heart, and I did just that. Maybe this is my karma for breaking her heart and leaving how I did.

I'm starting to believe that maybe Trinity and I aren't meant to be together. However, as soon as that thought comes to my head, I quickly shake it out. I know Trinity, and I are meant to be because she is a part of me. God made her from my rib. I just need for her to see that. However, one thing I'm not about to do is beg her to see that. Trinity will have to see that we are meant to be together on her own terms. Until then, I'm going to fall back and allow her to figure out what she wants.

If I ain't got you. . .

Trinity

"You have reached the voicemail of-" I ended the call. I've been calling Onyx for the last week and have yet to hear back from him. I haven't seen or heard from him since the night he left me in the truck. As soon as I said those words to him, I regret them. There was no way I would ever want to be back with Aiden. I just didn't like his tone of voice when he was talking to me. Questioning me as if I would call Aiden to come to my parents' house as if that man hadn't done what he did to me.

I went back to the house thinking that he would show up later that night and we can talk this out like adults but, when I woke that morning, I saw that he wasn't there, and neither was Damiana. I know what I said was wrong and out of pocket. I was just mad and upset over the entire situation with Aiden. I was confused as to how he could demand that I go with him, yet while we were together, he treated me like shit. Honestly, I shouldn't even have been mad at Onyx; it's the damn pregnancy that had my hormones all out of whack.

I waited two whole days before I went to his barbershop only to find out that he hadn't been there. His best friend Tanz told me he hadn't seen him since the last day I did. Just as I was about to go to the police, Tanz called me to pass along a message from Onyx.

I didn't even want to hear what he had to tell me at that

point. I mean, how disrespectful can he be. He didn't even have the decency to call me himself to tell me what he had to say. Even after I blew up his phone, he still didn't answer nor call me back.

I picked up my phone to call him again when I looked up and saw Kianna headed my way. I put Onyx's on the back burner and focused my attention on my friend. Kianna had called me last night, and I finally decided to answer. She wanted to bitch and complain about me, not talking to her. I was in no mood to discuss it over the phone and invite her out to lunch. Since Onyx wasn't around, this was the perfect time to grab some seafood. It's all I've been craving, and he refuses to allow me to eat it.

I stood from the table to greet my friend. "Kianna." As always, Kianna was dressed to the nine in designer clothing from head to toe. Make-up flawless as always and hair slayed.

"Hey-" Her words trailed, and her eyes grew wide when they fell to my stomach. "You're pregnant?" Her expression was hard to read. I didn't know whether if she was happy for me or upset. Knowing how much she hated Aiden, I'm sure is pissed.

I nodded. "Yes." I grabbed her hand. "Come sit down; I'll explain it all to you."

We both sat in the booth, "I have so much to tell you."

We quickly looked over the menu before the waitress came and took our order. We both ordered the seafood platter, and the waitress took our menus and left just as quickly as she came.

Kianna took a sip of her water. "Yeahhhhh, you do. You didn't say nothing about being pregnant on the phone last night. I thought I was your best friend." She pouted.

"Girl, stop, you know you're my best friend."

"Your best friend who you haven't talk to in months. I'm soooo hurt." I rolled my eyes at her dramatics. "So, what did Aiden have to say about that." She said, pointing at my round stomach. I instantly felt some type of way. I know Kianna doesn't like

Aiden but, that wouldn't have anything to do with my child.

"Um... about that, Aiden isn't my child's father." Her eyes grew wide.

"W-what? Well, who is?"

I opened my mouth to reply when a man walking into the restaurant caught my attention. My mouth fell open wide when I realized it was Onyx looking good as ever. Then I noticed that he wasn't alone. My eyes slid over to the woman who was standing next to him. She was tall, thin, with long blonde hair. I have never seen this woman before, and by the looks of how she was smiling at him, this must not be their first time together.

I closed my eyes and reopened them because I knew what I was seeing couldn't be real. I took a deep breath and counted to ten to keep my cool. The last thing I needed right now was to act out when I don't even know what's really going on.

I watched them laugh and talk as they waited on a table. Kianna was talking to me but, at this moment, whatever she was saying to me didn't matter. I needed to figure out who this woman is and why is Onyx with her.

I tried my hardest to focus my attention back on catching up with Kianna. I sat there on autopilot, just listening to her go on and on about her life while my focus was on Onyx and this mystery woman. I know I shouldn't even be mad because we aren't actually in a relationship. However, he should have thought about that before he started claiming my child. Before he started showing me how much he cared about me. That's before he made me fall for him.

Maybe I'm overreacting about the entire situation. That's what I told myself as I watched her reach over the table and wipe his mouth. The way he smiled at her is the same way he smiled at me. All the mental prep talk I gave myself went out as I stood from the table and made my way towards them.

They were so engrossed in their conversation that they

didn't even see me standing in front of the table. I finally got a better look at this woman, and she wasn't even all that cute. Her wig was matted at the top; her dress was faded, which meant it was old, and she had on way too much make up. Whoever, this woman is basic, and she can't even fuck with me on my worse day.

Clearing my throat to get their attention, they both looked up, and Onyx didn't seem the least bit bothered by me standing here.

"Hello, Trinity." He had the nerve to smile as if everything was okay. Showing off that one dimple I love.

"Hello, Trinity? Is that all you have to say to me? After I've been calling your phone for the last week? And where have you been you haven't been home either? Is she the reason why you haven't been home?" I yelled, not giving a fuck if I caused a scene for not.

"Um... No, I'm just his-" Onyx raised his hand, cutting her off.

"Excuse me, Evelyn." He stood from the table, grabbed my arm, and pulled me out of the restaurant. At this point, I could care less about causing a scene. He is going to have to explain to me just who this woman is supposed to be.

As soon as we walked out of the door, I yanked my arm away from him. "Don't touch me."

"Relax Trinity, yo' ass is stressing the baby."

"No, you're stressing the baby. You and Damiana haven't been home, nor have you been answering the phone." I pouted. I stared at him for a minute hoping that would move him, but it didn't. He stood there completely unbothered. I tried my hardest not to acknowledge how sexy he looked. The brown sweater and khaki pants he wore looked good against his mocha skin.

Shaking those thoughts out of my head, the last thing I need is to be blinded by lust. It's been so long since I have had these feelings for a man.

"What is it that you want Trinity I'm in the middle of something." No matter how much I try and act as if Onyx and I are only just friends. I have to be honest with myself I want more from him, I just don't know if I'm really ready for him.

I bit my bottom lip. As much as I didn't want to beg him, seeing him with that other woman is leaving me with no choice. "Onyx, can you just come home, please."

"Why?"

I narrowed my eyes at him. "What do you mean, why?"

He ran his hand down his face. "Why do you want me to come back huh? It's clear you made your choice that night with what you wanted to do. So, I'm giving you your space."

"I don't want space," I answered quickly.

"What do you want, Trinity?" Sighing loudly, I knew this was his way of getting me to tell him how I truly feel about him. I just hope once I express my feelings, he doesn't just treat me any differently.

"I want you to come home because I miss you and I want you-"

"Trinity!"

Both me and Onyx turned at the sound of my name being called. My eyes landed on Aiden, and my breath was instantly taken away. With each step that he took towards me, the flashback of what he did to me coming was on repeat in my mind. I don't know if I will ever be able to get over the things, he did to me.

How did he know I was here? Was the first question that came to my mind.

"Trinity, we need to talk!" Aiden stepped closer to me.

Onyx quickly stepped in front of me, pushing me behind him. "Nigga, didn't I tell you, Trinity is no longer your concern!"

"I'm not trying to hear that shit! Like I said, I need to speak to my fiancée so step of my way nigga."

"How is she your fiancée when she is my wife!" Onyx shout back.

My mouth fell wide open, hearing Onyx referring to me as his wife.

"Wife?" Aiden cut his eyes at me. "Is he the reason why you called the wedding off? Huh?" He moved in my direction, and Onyx pushed him back.

"Nigga, is you dumb? Address me, not my wife." Onyx spat. My nerves were bad, watching the two of them go at it.

"How is she your wife when it's my child growing in her belly-"

Wham!

Aiden didn't even finish his sentence when Onyx punched him hard in the face. That's when all hell broke loose, and they were both throwing hard blows at each other. I stood there in tears as I watched them go at it. Adding to the fact that I know I'm the reason they are fighting made me feel guilty as fuck.

"Trinity, what the hell is going on here? Is that Aiden? Who is he fighting?" I had completely forgot about Kianna being here. "Oh my God, is that Onyx fighting Aiden?" I ignored her questions when I saw a group of people gathering to watch the fight unfold. Not one person bothered to stop the fight.

The blaring sound of police sirens got my attention. The last thing I needed right now was for Onyx to go to jail. The police will take one look at his record and send him back without a second thought.

"Onyx, please! Stop the police is coming." I screamed.

He pushed Aiden to the ground. "Pussy ass nigga! Stay the fuck away from my wife." He quickly grabbed my arm and pulled me away. I looked back at Aiden on the ground, bruised, bloody, and felt no kind of remorse for his condition. He deserves a whole lot more than that. Especially after what he did to me.

"Trinity! Trinity!" Kianna called behind me.

"I'll call you!" I replied before Onyx shoved me into the car.

There was no time for me to tell her anything. We needed to get out of there before the police came.

Onyx sped out of the restaurant parking lot. He was driving so fast that I couldn't even get my seat belt on. "Slow down; I don't even got my seatbelt on!" I shouted.

My request fell on deaf ears as he continued to speed through the streets of Dallas. I said a quick prayer hoping that we made it back home in one piece. The car ride, all the way home was quiet, which meant that Onyx mind was ticking. I know he was probably wondering why Aiden showed up.

"Is this a new car?" I asked, trying to make small talk, hoping that he would take the bait. This black on black small SUV was cute, something more for a woman. When he didn't respond, I knew he was still pissed off.

I sat back in my seat and closed my eyes. I really hope he doesn't think that I have anything to do with why Aiden just showed up there. He already feels like for whatever reason that I want to be back with him when that is the furthers from the truth. My only concern is the well-fair of my child, and going back to Aiden would be the biggest mistake on my end.

The entire ride to the house was quiet. I wanted to ask him if he was going to pick up Damiana, but I figure he wanted to have alone time to discuss what just transpired.

He still has yet to explain the woman he was having lunch with. Also, we need to talk about why he claimed me as if his wife.

I want to know why would he say something like that when we aren't even in a relationship? Why would he say that when I don't even know if I'm ready to receive the love he is trying to give me.

We pulled up to the house, he quickly jumped out the car and made is way to my side of the car. He opened my door and helped me out of the car. As always, he cared about my well-being, if not anything else. I loved that about him.

Love? Where did that word come from? Is that how I actually truly feel?

Shaking away those thoughts for now. I don't know how to deal with those feelings right at this moment. Especially since he has yet to say anything to me. "Thank you," I told him, and he nodded. He turned around to walk away but, I grabbed his arm, stopping him. "Wait, can we talk?"

When he didn't bother to turn around to even look at me, it hurt my feelings. Damn, what did I do so bad to deserve this treatment?

"Onyx," I yelled, tugging on his arm. "Are you going to talk to me?" He finally turned to face me, and I stared into his eyes.

He grabbed my arm and led me towards the house. No words were exchanged; one of the things that I couldn't get about him was the fact that I couldn't read him. Following his lead, I walked behind him as we both entered the house. Closing the door behind me, I decided to just head up to my room.

It was clear that Onyx didn't have nothing to say to me, and I'm not about to sit here and just be ignored. If this is the was how things were about to be, I need to think about my future.

As I headed up the stairs, I stopped mid-way. A part of me just wanted to give up and just move on with my life. After dealing with Aiden's bullshit for all those years, I don't have the time or patience to push the issue of a relationship. However, a nagging feeling in my mind told me to go back and deal with Onyx. Talk to him figure things out with him. To try to see where head is at and if things can be fixed between us.

I turned around and headed back downstairs, running right into Onyx. His face still held a blank expression that was hard to read.

He let out a heavy sigh, "I'm sorry." He spoke first. I bit my lip as I stared into those deep, dark brown eyes. My heartbeat increased. "I'm sorry for not coming home. I'm sorry for not believing you bout Ol'dude. It's just, the thought of you going back to him fucked me up. I'm man enough to admit that. I know we have history together; I just want the chance to win back your heart."

Grabbing his hands, I lead towards him. "Aiden is the last thing on my mind. The shit that I endured with him has caused me to be a bit weary of who I let into my heart. I know you want a chance at my heart, and I want to give you that chance. However, I don't know if I'm ready for that just yet." I confessed. "I am willing to do the work on building with each other; I just need you to take things slow with me. Can you do that for me?"

"I'll do whatever it takes to make sure that you are mine. I love you not only for who you are, Trinity but for what I am when I'm with you. I don't even know how to explain it but, having you and Damiana here with me changed me for the better." He placed his hand on my round stomach. "Even though it wasn't my sperm that created this life, I'm going to be the man who raise her." He said with a wide smile.

Rolling my eyes playfully. "Really her? You just insist on having a girl, huh?"

"Damn right." Onyx pulled into his hard body and slammed his lips against mine. His kisses were rough, yet soft, which caused my body to melt in his arms. It's like my body and mind weren't on the same page. My body reacted the way I feel when I'm in his arms; meanwhile, my mind kept reminding me of the heartache I endured. I don't know how long it will take to get over this, all I do know is I'm willing to put in the work every day until I'm ready to open up my heart to him. I just hope is still around when the time comes.

Is it ever too late?

Aiden

Pacing back and forth in my kitchen, it was taking everything in me not to blow the fuck up. It's been three days since the shit went down at the restaurant. I have never in my life experience some shit like that before.

"Aiden calm down; let me look at your lip." My head snapped over to Kianna.

I scoffed. "Look at my lip for what?" I was fuming inside. Kianna ass is the reason why all this shit went down. Matter of fact, "Why the fuck did you come here?" I snapped at her. She called me this morning say she wanted to talk but, all she has done since she's got here was get on my damn nerves.

"I'm here for my money. The fuck. Did you not forget our deal?" She laughed.

"Your money?" I hissed.

"Yes, the money you owe me for getting Trinity to the restaurant now, pay the fuck up."

Something snapped in my head, and I instantly blacked out. When I came to, I had my hands wrapped around her neck tightly. "Bitch yo' ass won't get not another dime from me. Matter of fact, sign the fuckin' divorce papers so I can finally be done with yo' ass!" I barked.

She clawed at my hands to get me to let her loose. "A-Aiden, please." I watched tears build in her eyes, and I didn't feel one ounce of sympathy for her. For years Kianna has been a pain in my ass! I regret the damn day I married her ass. The first mistake I ever made in my life. The second one being; losing Trinity.

I squeezed tighter. "Please, what, huh? I'm sick of your shit! You haven't been worth shit since the day I met you." I watched her face turn a dark shade of red. I had half of mind to choke her to death. I removed my hands from her neck, and she instantly started gasping for air. "Get the fuck out, Kianna. The next time I see you better be when you sign the divorce papers."

"Aiden, I will not sign them papers." I froze at Kianna's voice. I slowly turned around to face her.

"You either sign them papers or-"

"Or what?" She challenged. "What you go do to me that you haven't already done? Huh? After everything you've done to me you, think that paying my bills just makes everything alright? No, not even close. You owe me so much more."

I scoffed. "I owe you?" I asked for clarification because I couldn't have heard her correctly.

"Yes, you owe me for everything you put me through-"

"Kianna, get the fuck out!" I barked, cutting her off. I'd had enough of this back and forth with her.

"I'm not going nowhere, Aiden; haven't you realized that by now?" She crossed the kitchen and stood in front of me. Kianna's beauty was undeniable; however, the bullshit that came with her blocked that out. "Even when we both went our sperate ways somehow, someway we were brought back together. You and Trinity's relationship didn't work, don't you see why? We are made to be together."

Before I could protest, Kianna pushed her lips against mine. It was sudden, and I wanted to push her away from me, but there was something about this kiss. "I still love you, Aiden, even after all these years." The passion I felt behind the kiss threw me off. It's been years since I've been intimate with Kianna. I didn't have no clue she still felt the same way about me. "I don't even blame you anymore for the miscarriage. I know now that I wasn't the right time to bring a child into this world. I just want us to be able to start over, and if it doesn't work this time, then I will grant you the divorce." She stated.

I heard everything Kianna said, I just didn't know how to take it. When we married, we were young and dumb; I was not ready to be a husband. Hell, I wasn't even ready to be someone's boyfriend. Yet, I took advantage of Kianna's heart. I honestly never gave her a chance to be my wife. Maybe the reason Trinity and I didn't work out is because my soul was already one with another. If Kianna and I are going to start in a fresh note, I need to be honest with myself and her.

Wrapping my arms around Kianna, I pulled her closer to me. "I need to be honest for a moment, Kianna." I lead her over to the kitchen table. "I still love Trinity very much, and what you're looking for is something I can't give you. I owe you that much."

Tears fell freely from her eyes. "Just give me a chance; you never really given me that. Please, Aiden." I pained me to hear her beg, which isn't Kianna's style, to begin with.

I opened my mouth to speak when the sound of someone clapping caught our attention. I turned around, and my mouth fell wide open when my eyes on Trinity. My mouth went dry, and I worried of how much she had heard. Like I just explain to Kianna. I still loved Trinity with all my heart, and if I had any chance of getting back with her, I'll do anything to do it.

I stood from the table and rushed to her. Even dressed in a plain tee and sweatpants, I could see her beauty. Pregnancy looked good on her. It's just what I imagined that she would look like carrying my children. "Trinity baby-"

She took a step back and looked in between both me and Kianna. Then she walked over to the table and sat down in front of her. Looking at Kianna's face, I could tell she was just as surprised as me.

"Trinity friend, let me explain," Kianna said softly.

"Please go right ahead. Aiden come to have a seat; let's all have a friendly chat." Trinity spoke calmly.

I looked over at Kianna, who was just as confused as I was. Wasting no more time, I went and sat at the table.

Taking a deep breath, I prepared myself for this chat as Trinity called it. I knew deep down that things will be far from 'friendly.'

All Secrets Soon Come To Light...

Kianna

I sat in front of my best friend of over ten years, with tears burning to escape my eyes. This is something I never wanted to do. I never wanted to explain to my friend that the man she has loved and been engaged to has always been my husband. I remember how happy she was with him when they first met. As a friend, I knew how long she had been unhappy, so who was I to stand between her and her happiness?

She looked at me, and I could tell that she was hurt by my actions. It hurt me to see her hurt whether she knows it or not. I do love her, and never in a million years did I ever want to hurt her. She doesn't deserve it.

She chuckled and shook her head. "Kianna, friend. Please tell me this ain't true. Are you and Aiden married?" I heard a hint of sadness in her voice. The tears that I was holding at bay finally escaped.

My voice was caught in my throat, that I couldn't even answer her. All I could do was nod.

"Wow." Was her only response. "After all these years, you didn't think that you could have shared that information, huh?"

"Listen-" She raised her hand, stopping me.

"You know what." She paused, then stood from the table. "I don't even care. Kianna, you and Aiden are both grown, plus at the end of the day, y'all are husband and wife. What I have to say doesn't even matter when it comes to that."

I stood from the table. "No, wait, you have to hear me out first."

"No. I rather not. I'm almost due, and the last thing I need is to be stressed by two people who no longer matter in my life." Hearing those words come out, her mouth hurt me like I'd been shot in the chest. The fact she said I didn't matter felt like arm was taken from my lungs.

"Trinity believe when I say I never meant for things to go this far. Please, you are all I have."

She scoffed. "I'm not, though. You have your husband." She pointed over at Aiden. My eyes met his, and he was just as fucked up about this as I was. Trinity both meant something to us, and neither one of us wanted to hurt her intentionally.

"You want to know what's really fucked up about all this is? You were the main one telling me to leave Aiden and how he wasn't no good for me. Meanwhile, you just wanted him for yourself, ain't that right?"

I couldn't even respond because half of what she was saying is true. I did want her to leave Aiden because he wasn't no good for her. He'd did her the same as he done me, and as my friend, I knew she deserves more.

"I was trying to save you from the same mistake I made all those years ago."

"Right. So, I'm just supposed to sit back and act as if I did hear you begging for another chance at y'all marriage?" I didn't have no come back. "Nothing to say, huh? Just like I thought."

"Look, I know you're upset, and you have every right to be just don't let this come between us. We've been friends for over ten years. We can move past this." I tried to reason with her.

Trinity and I have been through some shit together as friends that we have both come back from. There is no reason why we could get past this as well. I mean, I know with time we could, I just don't want to end our friendship.

"Had this have been a little disagreement or something minor of that sort, then yes, we could have moved past this. However, you and Aiden being married is a whole different thing. The fact you were going to stand next to me on my wedding day as I said vows to your husband and not say nothing is the dumbest shit I could even imagen. I mean, come on now how was it even going to work. I guess you wanted him to be married to the both of us so you can have his arrest for bigamy. Is that what you wanted?"

I was trying my hardest to keep my composure with Trinity but, what she was saying was downright insulting.

"Look, you are just doing the most right now. Try to be reasonable." I hissed.

With wide eyes, Trinity stepped closer to me. "Be reasonable, are you serious? How can I be reasonable when the people I trusted the most betrayed me? Like all this time, I thought you was being a friend; you weren't doing nothing but being a sneaky hating ass bitch! You were just mad that Aiden wanted me. You were jealous of what we had together. He loves me and will always love me, which is something he will never ever do for you." She barked. Hearing her say that, I lost it. Friends or not, she had crossed the line and had me fucked up.

I walked up to her, reached back, and punched her dead in her fucking mouth. "Bitch, fuck you! You don't know my life!" I shouted as I began to punch her all over.

"Kianna, what the fuck!" Aiden shouted as he tried to pull me off her. "Kianna, she's pregnant!" Hearing that only made me madder. I was blinded by rage, and Trinity was going to be my outlet. I didn't give a fuck about her or her baby for the first time in a long time; I focused on myself and how I felt.

Trinity has always acted as if she was perfect when she is far from it. She has her own secrets. She wanted to act as if she wasn't pregnant with Aiden's baby, but I knew better. I knew my best friend. She tried to act as if her baby belongs to Onyx; I knew different. That is Aiden's child, and she is wrong for what she is doing, not allowing that man a chance to be a father. And she has the nerve to call me sneaky.

Pow!

Pow!

The sound of a gunshot made me stop mid-swing. Turning around, my eyes laid on Onyx hold a 9mm aimed directly at me.

"Back the fuck up from my wife before I empty the clip inside you." I moved away from Trinity a moved closer to Onyx. Seeing him with that gun in his hand pointed at me caused something to snap inside my head. The fact that death was so near,

"Go ahead and shot me. I ain't got shit to live for anymore anyway." Everything that has transpired today made me realize that I don't have no one in my life. The pain I felt in my heart, I couldn't even describe it. Trinity and I aren't no longer friends, and according to Aiden, he doesn't even want to give us another try. I literally have no one else in this world. My family cut me off years ago, so who do I have?

"Come on, Kianna, you need to calm down." Aiden tried to pull me away, but I snatched away from him.

"Get your hands off me!" I snatched away from Aiden and walked closer to Onyx. "Come one-shot me! I know how niggas like you are. You don't pull a gun out unless you're going to use it, right? So, use it!"

Onyx dropped the gun and put it back into his pocket. "Kianna, you need to calm down." He suggested.

I scoffed. "Calm down? Nigga, fuck you!" I launched at him and began to punch him all over.

Aiden came from behind me and grabbed me. "Calm the fuck down!" He growled in my ear.

I opened my mouth to curse him out when a loud scream came from Trinity. "My water broke."

At the same time, Onyx and Aiden both ran to her aide. My eyes began to water as I watched them tend to her. It made me realize that I will never have that. No one will ever care for me the way I deserve.

It hurts to love someone and not be loved in return. But what is more painful is to love someone and never find the courage to let that person know how you feel. For years I sat back and hid my true feeling about how I felt about Aiden. I allowed my hate for him to mask my real feelings for him. Now, seeing him at Trinity's aide being so caring and attentive, I know that he will never ever feel the same way for me.

Grabbing my bag, I made my way towards the door. I looked back to get another glimpse of my best friend and husband because this will be the last time I see them. When the thoughts of dying came to play in my head, that's when I realize that this entire situation is unhealthy. No matter what is going on, I have to live the life I was given. Turning around, I walked out of the house and away from the life I once knew. I will be signing the divorce papers and sending them right over to Aiden. In order for me to be happy, I have to let go of this life.

Trinity

"Ahhh!" I cried as another contraction hit me. I can't believe that my water broke. I'm only thirty-two weeks along, which means my baby is early. If I could stand up, I would beat the shit out of Kianna for doing this to me. Never in a million years would I expect my so-called 'friend' to do this to me.

No matter what happened between us, I would never lay hands on her while she was pregnant. Honestly, even if she wasn't pregnant, I still wouldn't lay hands on her. Even though both her and Aiden were in the wrong, my fight was never with her.

My mama always taught me check the man, never the bitch. I laid next to Aiden every night. It was him who I was about to vow in front of good for the rest of my life with. If Kianna didn't come clean, he should have. True I knew her longer than him. However, he was supposed to be my friend, my lover, and lifetime partner; it was his responsibility to tell me the real.

"Baby, what's wrong, what do you need." I heard Aiden say. I opened my mouth to go off on him, but another contraction hit me.

"Get the fuck off of her," Onyx yelled. I caught the look of rage on Onyx's face. I knew it was practically because I left the house telling him I was going shopping for the baby and ended up here.

I'm glad he came because there is no telling how much damage Kianna would have done to me if he wasn't here.

Groaning as another contraction hit me. I need to get to a hospital asap. The last thing is to have this baby right here on the kitchen floor.

"Please get me to the hospital," I begged Onyx.

"I got you, baby," He swooped me into his arm and walked out the kitchen.

Click!

The sound of a gun cocking stopped him in his tracks. He turned to see Aiden aiming a gun at us.

My heartbeat increased as I stared into Aiden's eyes. His face had the same psychotic look in his eyes the night he beat and raped me. "Trinity, I can't let you leave with him. You are mine, and if I can't have you, then..." His words trailed off as he aimed the gun directly at Onyx.

"Please, Aiden don't do this," I begged.

His eyes widen. "Are you really begging for his life?" He hissed.

"Man, fuck this." I heard Onyx say before he turned to walk away.

Pow!

Pow!

The two bullets hit Onyx, causing both of us to fall to the ground. Onyx groaned in pain. I knew he was hit, but I couldn't see where.

"ONYX!!!" I cried.

Everything was happening so fast I didn't expect none of this to happen. I came here to have a conversation with Aiden about our child because after thinking about it, I could keep this away from him. Deep down, I knew that this baby meant so much to him. Now I was regretting this entire thing.

"You see Trinity," Aiden said as he walked closer to me with the gun aim directly at my head. "I have always loved you. Even when I thought I was over you and moved on, you came back to be carrying our princess. I am sorry for everything I have ever done to you. Just promise me that when our daughter as about me, you tell her nothing but great things."

Tears poured from my eyes because I knew what he was trying to tell me. I opened my mouth to speak just as Aiden put the gun into his mouth and pulled the trigger.

Pow!!!

Epilogue

Four Months Later. . .

Trinity

Soft cries coming from the baby monitor caught my attention. Throwing the cover back, I got out of bed to tend to my fussy baby girl. "Nah, I got her. Go back to sleep." Onyx said as he jumped out of bed to tend to Audrey.

I didn't even put up a fight like I usually do. I got back in bed and snuggled under the covers. With Audrey not sleeping through the night, I find myself more tired than ever now.

Being a mom to a newborn, a stepmom to a pre-teen, and a wife. Yep. Onyx and I have been officially married for about three weeks now. A little over a month ago, he had to undergo major surgery to remove the bullet that was had broken inside of his thigh.

The doctors said that there would be a possibility that he would lose his leg, and with Onyx in the middle of a custody battle with his baby mama, he didn't want to lose Damiana, and neither did I. Which lead us to get married. At first, I thought it was too soon; I did it anyway for the sake of our family. I knew I loved Onyx; at the same time, I didn't know if I was ready for the whole 'marriage' part.

Even though I always imagined myself having this big fancy wedding. Honestly, I didn't expect nothing less than that. However, I settled for a small ceremony at the courthouse with just myself, Onyx, the girls, and my parents. Although it was something I never planned on happening, it was the second happiest day of my life. The first being the day I had Audrey.

The day I had Audrey was a day full of emotions. All I mostly remember about that day was going to the hospital cover in Aiden's blood. Aiden rests his soul shot himself in front of me and shot Onyx twice. Once in the arm and his thigh. I was in shock; my blood pressure was through the roof, sending me into an emergency C-section for the sake of Audrey. I can't even describe my feelings at that point. I was ready to just give up and say fuck everything. Aiden was dead, and I didn't even know what was going on with Onyx.

That was until I saw my baby girl's face. All I could do was cry tears of joy. Then it hit me; my daughter was born the same day her father died. I cried so hard. How would I explain that to her when she gets older and ask for father? Then I learned that Onyx survived. He came in like my superman putting his on recover on the back burning and focusing on both me and Audrey. He wasting no time signing Audrey's birth certificate and giving her his last name.

At first, I was kind of skeptical about it because I didn't know how Aiden's family would feel about that. Then his rude, dry wig wearing mama took one look at Audrey and swore she wasn't Aiden's daughter. All she cared about was her son's money and his 'good' name. At first, I was hurt, then Onyx reassured me that Audrey will be taken care of no matter what. That's when I knew that I loved Onyx, and he was the man for me.

Our relationship has been so refreshing. Onyx made me fall in love with him every day. Our relationship is far from perfect, but we both work on it like it's a job. When we have a disagreement about something, we both take the time to listen to each other. We discuss it, fix it, and move on.

Honestly, over the last few months for me has been life changing. I went from being in an abusive relationship to a loving marriage. My hope was that when I found love again, I prayed that it was everything that I dreamed about. That I would find a love that has power to tear down the painful walls of my past relationship with Aiden, and Onyx did just that.

Onyx came in filled my heart with so much love. I learned to trust, communicate, and understand on levels that I never had with Aiden. He made sure I felt safe and protected at all times. He helped me work through my flaws, helped my growth, and evolve in ways I never thought I could in such a short period of time.

"Trin baby, you sleep?" I rolled over to see my sexy husband holding our sleeping daughter on his chest. Even with the scar on his shoulder from where the bullet hit him, he was sexy as ever.

"No." I shook my head, pointing at them. "She is not getting in the bed with us."

Onyx wide smile showed that one sexy dimple that I love. "Why you trying to make my son tonight?"

"SON? I'm not having no more kids. Audrey is enough."

He scoffed. "Right." He got into the bed with Audrey still on his chest. My baby girl has her poor daddy wrapped around her finger, and Onyx doesn't care. "I want my son, Trinity, and I'm going to get him."

I bit my lip because I know he was telling the truth. I love my husband, and I'll give him whatever he wants, even if that meant giving him a house full of kids. I guess that's the price of being made to love a thug.

THE END.

Traniqua Francis was born and raised in Galveston, Texas. The twenty-eight-year-old is a single mother to a beautiful, very spoiled thirteen-year-old little girl.
The author started writing poems at the young age of nine years old. It wasn't until her early twenties she began to write novels to cope with her depression and anxiety.
The author now has seventeen books under her pen with more to come

Follow the author on Facebook, Twitter, and Instagram: TraNiquaTheAuthor